I0587619

Home Runs, Double Plays, & SPIES

Also Available From Elizabeth Lee Sorrell

Wrong Turn Fairy Tales

Exclusively available on
Barnes & Nobles for Nook Book.

More Than Instinct

Black & White

Red and the Big Bad...

Wolf?

Available from your favorite bookstores.

The Clause Rebellion

Attack On the Clause

His Christmas Star

Her Second Chance

Home Runs, Double Plays, & SPIES

Elizabeth LEE Sorrell

Yarbrough House Publishing, Inc.

AcKNOWLEDGEments

I'd like to thank my family who really do all the hard work. While I sit back and make up fanciful stories, my family stays busy proofing, formatting, illustrating, crunching numbers, and taking care of all the "business stuff." All I do is play with my imagination, but my family works hard to bring life to my stories.

Chapter One

Lindsey was not on good terms with her boss, Dan Scad. In a small town you knew everyone, and Dan and Lindsey grew up in a very small town called Forest Hills. They had been rivals for as long as they could remember. They did not have any real reason to dislike each other. They just always had. It started back in preschool. Lindsey wanted to play ball with the boys. Dan did not want any girls to play, and that was all it took. Dan and Lindsey would never get along after that day.

They were very competitive with one another. In every aspect of their lives they made it their goal to outdo the other. Their grades soared as they pushed themselves higher and higher. They put in late hours and early mornings studying.

They were outstanding employees. They were always on time and very hard workers. Their productivity was outstanding simply because they each wanted to do more than the other. In some ways they were good for each other, but in other ways... not so much.

On the school newspaper, they were the two best writers due to their competition. They were always trying to one up the other and get all the best stories to report. They would read and reread their articles as many times as it took before turning them in. The last thing either of them wanted was to make a grammar mistake or a typo that the other had not.

Sports, however, were the biggest pain, because in those moments they let themselves outwardly show their competitiveness more. They became more aggressive, sometimes intentionally targeting each other. Winning became everything, but winning wasn't enough. They each wanted to be the team hero who pushed the team to victory. Losing? Well, losing just wasn't an option.

Dan and Lindsey are all grown up now, and still opposing one another. Dan and Lindsey work for the town's local newspaper Sun Times. Dan is editor and chief. Lindsey is a journalist. Dan's father pulled some strings to get him his job. Lindsey, on the other hand, worked hard to learn her job. She earned her position, and Dan makes her work for it every step of the way.

He loved making her miserable. Lindsey gets stuck with all the grunt work. Any pieces that no one else wanted went straight to Lindsey. Pieces that were almost too boring to even print also went to Lindsey. She was his escape goat in a sense.

As Lindsey Sanders walked into the conference room, she could not believe she was writing up another FBI update. Those FBI updates were so boring. Nothing ever changed. How did a small town like Forrest Hills end up on the FBI's radar anyway? How many places large or small got regular updates from an actual FBI spokesman? There had to be an interesting past connecting Forrest Hills to the FBI. Now, that would make for a great article, except Dan had shot it down multiple times already.

What made FBI reports worse was that the FBI's spokesperson, Brandon Cobb, was not very pleasant himself. He always had a scowl on his face. It was obvious that he did not want to be there any more than Lindsey.

Questions only seemed to annoy him even though that was what he was there for. Conversation aggravated him. He had a never ending supply of smart comments. He was quick tempered and short on manners. The saying "Don't judge a book by its cover" rang true with Mr. Cobb too.

To call him nice looking was a gross understatement. He had dark hair, dark skin, and dark eyes. He was just over six feet and in perfect shape. No artist could have sculpted a better physique. His dark hair was always neatly in place. His golden brown complexion was absolutely mesmerizing. You could easily get lost in his big, brown eyes if you were not careful. There were very few physical flaws on Brandon Cobb. He was a positively gorgeous man. Tall, dark, and handsome fit him perfectly.

Maybe if they had met under different circumstances, things could have gone very differently. Then again, as soon as he opened his mouth, that would be spoiled too. There was no argument that he was good looking. It was too bad his overall personality made him so revolting. He could have been a good catch. It wasn't fair that someone so beautiful could be so sour.

"Hi, Mr. Cobb, how are you today?" Lindsey asked politely.

"Let's just get this over with, Sanders. I've got better things to do than answer questions all day," Brandon shot back.

"Sure thing, Mr. Cobb. There were rumors last week of elevated terrorist activity. What can you tell me in regards to such rumors?"

"Nothing. I have no information on that at this time."

"There were also rumors of a possible terrorist attack," Lindsey pushed.

"I have no information on that at this time," Brandon responded quickly.

"What about the rumors of terrorist activity right here in Forest Hills?" Lindsey insisted. The very idea was absurd. What would be the point of hitting such a small target. Still, Lindsey would take anything she could get at this point, if only Cobb would say anything at all.

"Look, Sanders, you said it yourself. They are rumors. A few too many house wives with nothing better to do sat around talking too much. I have no information on terrorist anything at this time. Now skip over the terrorist bull before I die of old age," Brandon groused.

"Of course, Mr. Cobb. Can you tell me anything about the kidnapping over in Atlanta last week?" Lindsey questioned.

"There are two suspects in custody at this time for questioning," Brandon replied.

"Do you have names and how they were connected to the girl?"

"I have no information on that at this time," Brandon responded predictably.

"Does the FBI believe the young girl to still be alive?" Lindsey inquired undeterred.

"I don't have that information at this time," he repeated.

"Ok. Moving right along. Is the FBI investigating the bomb threat on Forest Hills High this past Monday?"

"The FBI has no reason to believe that the threat was anything more than a local prank. The local authorities are handling Monday's bomb threat. Are we through, Sanders?" Brandon asked.

"I don't know. Is that all the information you have at this time Mr. Cobb?".

"Yeah, it is," Brandon answered shortly.

"Then I guess we're done here. Thank you for your time, Mr. Cobb."

Brandon rolled his eyes and left.

This would be another short article. Lindsey had been with the Sun Times eight years, and it was always the same old thing. Nothing worth reporting ever happened in Forest Hills, and Brandon Cobb rarely had any answers other than "I have no information on that at this time." Lindsey quickly wrote up her article and took it to Dan. Dan approved it right away. It was not much there to look over, and it wasn't like anyone was going to read it anyway.

Lindsey hurried home to see the baseball game. Lindsey was a big Atlanta Braves fan. She rarely missed a game, and living only one hour outside Atlanta, Lindsey went to as many home games as she could. She always followed the Braves season very closely. Lindsey was sort of the town's baseball expert. Lindsey loved to watch the games with Mr. Parks.

Mr. Parks was an older gentleman. He was well respected in the community, and he was the only one who loved the Atlanta Braves almost as much as Lindsey.

Mr. Parks was the owner of the Sun Times and Dan's great uncle. Mr. Parks' generosity toward family is the only reason Dan started out as editor and chief. Mr. Parks was also the only reason Dan cannot let Lindsey go from the Sun Times. Mr. Parks thought a great deal of Lindsey, and Lindsey thought a great deal of him. They had always had baseball in common. Mr. Parks taught Lindsey to play and coached her the entire way through little league, sometimes on a team with Dan and sometimes as an opponent.

Mr. Parks didn't have any children of his own, so he sort of adopted Lindsey as his own. Lindsey's own dad never had time for things like coaching little league. The demands on a cop could be time consuming even for a cop in a small town, one like Lindsey's dad.

Just after high school Lindsey's parents were killed in a car accident. Lindsey had no more family in Forest Hills or in Georgia for that matter. Mr. Parks took her under his wing. He taught her everything he knew about journalism and gave her a job at the Sun Times. Lindsey took what Mr. Parks taught her and blossomed into quite the young journalist.

Mr. Parks hated the way Dan worked Lindsey, but he could not fire him. He was family after all. Instead, Mr. Parks would play up Lindsey's talent to Dan and push to move Lindsey up in the ranks. It never worked. If anything, it made Dan more antagonistic, but Lindsey would never discourage Mr. Parks, not for the world.

Mr. Parks and Lindsey had lunch together every Sunday after church. It was sort of a special time that they shared together, and it had been a tradition for several years.

"Lindsey, I want to talk to you about something. I think you'll be excited. I'm working on making a deal with the Braves to have a full time reporter from the Sun Times to travel with the team as sort of a team reporter. I don't know a bigger Braves fan than you. Would you be interested in the position?" Mr. Parks asked.

"Would I be interested? Mr. Parks, you know I would. A chance like that would be a dream come true for me. I can't believe this! I must be dreaming! Mr. Parks, are you sure you want me? You could find so many wonderful reporters if you wanted. Are you sure?"

"Well of course, I'm sure. Don't be ridiculous. You're a wonderful reporter yourself, and no one could do a better job reporting the Braves than you. I want a true fan, someone who is genuinely interested in the games and the team to cover this," Mr. Parks insisted.

Lindsey was flattered. It was a dream position, and no one knew better than Mr. Parks how much it would mean to her. They both also knew that she never would have stood a chance at the position if it had been left up to Dan.

It was out of character for Mr. Parks to go above Dan's head. He didn't believe in strong arming people. He was simply too kind a man for that sort of thing. Just the fact alone that Mr. Parks would go over Dan's head meant a lot to Lindsey.

Mr. Parks was someone who loved her and looked out for her. They may not have been blood, but he was family, the only family she had left.

Chapter Two

The deal did go through, and Lindsey started right away. Dan was furious when he heard the job had already been promised to Lindsey, but Lindsey was not worried about Dan Scad anymore. The job was hers, and there was nothing he could do about it. Lindsey would not even have to look Dan in the face anymore. She was supposed to e-mail her reports into the station from here on out.

Lindsey loved her new position. She watched all the games live, and she got to write about something she really enjoyed. Baseball and writing were Lindsey's two favorite past times. She could not have been happier. The players and coaches were all very nice. They loved to joke around, smile, and have fun. Lindsey traveled with the team and reported on the games for the remainder of the season.

During the off season, Lindsey came home to Forest Hills, spending all her free time with Mr. Parks. Lindsey loved telling Mr. Parks all her baseball stories from that season, and Mr. Parks loved hearing them. Mr. Parks' favorite part was all the coaching tid bits and managing strategies.

Lindsey's favorite part was how down to earth the players were. She had halfway expected to meet a team full of super stars with big heads, but what she found was quite the contrary. They were all level headed, and great to talk baseball with. They were not too good to talk with Lindsey either.

One thing that Lindsey and Mr. Parks could agree on was how exciting the games were. That was one part of Lindsey's job that could never get old.

All winter long, they talked baseball. It was baseball year round; what could have been better?

Somedays Lindsey and Mr. Parks would meet up at a local coffee shop just to talk. The coffee was rich, smooth, and most importantly hot. The coffee shop had comfortable furniture with a cozy, welcoming environment. Plus, it was usually pretty quiet during normal working hours. That was another thing that Lindsey loved about her new position. She didn't keep regular hours during winter; in fact, she put in minimal hours during the winter. This meant less Dan Scad and more Mr. Parks.

"I especially liked the piece you did on Clint Peters and his mother," Mr. Parks mentioned one chilly day while the two of them were tucked nice and warm in the coffee shop.

"That was the sweetest article for Mother's Day weekend," Lindsey agreed.

"You hear so many of the players talk about how their dads coached them from little league and up or about the imperative role of an influential coach along the way. You don't hear too many stories about the role mom played."

"I hope it served as an inspiration for other single moms," Lindsey said wistfully. Clint Peters had grown up in a single parent home, just him, his older brother, and his mom. His dad had left not long after Clint was born, never to be heard from again. Clint's mom worked, raised two boys on her own, and taught her boys how to play baseball. Some players called their dads for help when they hit a slump; Clint Peters called his mom. She is an amazing woman, just as sweet and kind as she is strong and hard working. Lindsey had gotten to interview both Clint and his mom for the article, and it was truly heartwarming. "I hope I did their story justice."

"It was a touching article. It was a prime example of just why I wanted you for the job. You know the game of baseball. You cover what happens on the field like a pro, but it is more than just that. You capture the heart and soul of the team as a whole. A team is made up of more than simply what they do on the field; what they do off the field is just as important to who they really are."

"I can't even begin to tell you how much the Braves do for the community."

"Oh, I know, and thanks to you many others know now too. It's good that the kids looking up to the players know how well rounded the players are too."

As soon as spring training started up, Lindsey returned ready to meet all new staff and old. Lindsey waited patiently for the new outfielder. His story should be an interesting one. He had come out of nowhere, literally. He hadn't played in the minors, and no one had heard his name associated with professional baseball before.

Lindsey had been told that this was Kevin Baxter's first season in baseball since college. Lindsey could not wait to hear how the twenty-seven year old decided to get back into baseball and how he got invited to the Braves' spring training so soon. That was a long time to go without any formal involvement with baseball. It was odd that someone could get back into baseball professionally, much less make it to the show right off the bat. It wasn't just odd; it was unheard of. This guy must have really been something else.

Lindsey could not believe her eyes! Four men walked out onto the field wearing spring training uniforms. She recognized each one. She recognized the second baseman, the center fielder, and the catcher. The fourth man she recognized as Brandon Cobb, the spokesperson for the FBI, but there was no Brandon Cobb on any of the rosters that Lindsey had received.

Lindsey was nobody's fool; in fact, she was pretty bright. She usually caught on to things rather quickly. Brandon Cobb must have been going by a different name, and if he was going by a different name, you could be sure he did not want anyone to know it. Undercover work couldn't be easy. As far as Lindsey knew, her dad had never done any type of undercover work during all his years on the force. Still...

"Hi. I'm Lindsey Sanders," Lindsey said reaching out to shake his hand. He looked almost surprised at first, almost. You would have thought someone from the FBI could control their show of emotions better than that, especially if they were working undercover, which Brandon must have been.

"Hey Lindsey, I'm Kevin Baxter. How are you?" he asked.

Wow! He was being so polite that Lindsey was caught off guard for a second. She stuttered a little before catching herself. "I'm doing great. Thank you. Mr. Baxter, I work for a small town newspaper in Forest Hills. I was wondering if you would mind talking with me for just a minute."

"Call me Kevin. To tell you the truth, Lindsey, I was about to go warm up. Maybe we could grab a bite to eat after the game this afternoon. We could talk then if that's ok with you," Kevin offered.

"That sounds good. Where and when?".

"I'll meet you outside the club house after I shower and get changed. We can ride together," Kevin said.

"Great. I'll see you then," Lindsey replied.

The players were all so friendly that it was not unheard of for her to eat out with a few of them from time to time while doing interviews. Usually, though, she ate with a group of them or even their families. She had never gone out with one of the players one on one, but what was truly unusual was riding together. Then again, everything about this situation was going to be unusual.

This was going to be interesting, huh? What an understatement. Not only had he not played since college, but he worked for the FBI.

Lindsey met Kevin after the game just as scheduled. "This is me," he said pointing to a bright blue pickup truck, a beautiful blue but not one that you saw on cars very often. It was darker than the ocean but just as clear and pure. If she had to pick a crayola to match the color, Lindsey would have chosen cerulean. It was a real nice truck, and it was a real tall truck. A lot of money had gone into fixing that truck up.

Kevin helped Lindsey into the truck. To tell the truth, if he hadn't helped her, she would have needed a step stool; the truck tires were that tall.

They were quiet until they got out of the parking lot. Then in a harsh voice Kevin asked, "Why did you do it?"

"Why did I do what?" Lindsey responded.

"Don't play games with me. You know full well who I am, and we don't exactly get along. Why didn't you rat me out, Sanders?" Kevin demanded.

"Just because I don't respect you doesn't mean that I don't respect the job you do," Lindsey answered hotly.

"Is that right?"

"Yeah, my dad was a cop."

"What does that prove?"

"It wasn't always an easy job. I remember talking about how they all had each others back. It wasn't an every man for himself kind of job. It went further even than just his partner. They all had to look out for one another. I'm sure that things are different working on a federal level, but I'm betting that having each other's back transcends. Because I respect the job, I would never knowingly blow a man's cover."

"Fair enough," Kevin relented.

They rode in silence the rest of the way. "Look. I thought I was coming to get an interview with Kevin Baxter. If you have nothing to say, I'd prefer you take me back now," Lindsey said.

"What do you want to know?" Kevin asked.

"I had planned to ask how you decided to get back into baseball and how you got invited to spring training. Do you have a story to tell or do you not have any information on that at this time?"

"Oh, I've got your story alright. Let me come around and help you out. Sanders, don't jump," Kevin pleaded, but before he could get around the truck Lindsey had already jumped down.

"I can handle myself, Mr. Baxter, but thank you," she said.

"Whatever, just call me Kevin," he said sounding annoyed.

"I'm sure I'll remember that better once you realize that I don't go by Sanders," Lindsey returned.

After they ordered, Lindsey looked at Kevin waiting. "What's your problem?" he asked.

"You said you had a story to tell," Lindsey reminded him.

"I ought to have you sent back to Forest Hills," Kevin threatened.

"You wouldn't. You couldn't," Lindsey dared.

"I would, and I could," Kevin responded.

"Mr. Parks wouldn't hear of it," Lindsey informed him.

"Mr. Parks would not have a choice," Kevin told her.

"You can't do that. Dan would put me back on FBI reports," Lindsey said almost desperate now.

"I can, but I'll wait. You didn't rat me out today, but if you so much as think about a tell all session, girly, your bags are as good as packed," Kevin whispered.

"I can assure you I have no intentions of telling anything. All I want is an interview."

"You want to hear my story, huh. I was a personal trainer in south Alabama for the past six years, but I was bored. I wanted a change of pace. I enjoyed baseball growing up. I thought it might be more up my alley. I made a name for myself back in college. There were a lot of people who thought I'd go pro. I disappeared instead. I became a nobody, but I kept in shape and kept up my skills. I guess when I tried out the scouts had good things to say. The next thing I knew I was on my way to spring training. I mean to work hard now that I'm here. I'm looking to hopefully make a place for myself on this team," he explained.

"That's it?"

"Yeah, that's it. What were you expecting?" Kevin responded.

"I don't know. I guess I was expecting this elaborate, exciting story. How it was an up hill struggle to the top, or how bad you missed baseball. Maybe how you had everyone's full attention at tryouts because you were so good," she described.

"I'm a ball player. I'm not superman."

"Well, you must have done something amazing at tryouts. Someone had to see something in you. You had someone's attention. As of right now you're on the starting roster. As far as I know, you've never played at a minor league level. That's just not done," Lindsey insisted.

"I must have had good teachers. What's the big deal?" Kevin asked.

"What's the big deal? You're the big deal. You're doing the impossible. You are becoming a living legend."

"Don't do that. Don't blow this out of proportion. I'm just a ball player trying to make it to the majors. It doesn't need all that dramatization," Kevin said.

"Well, I guess if that's the way you want it," Lindsey backed down. She did not know why Brandon/Kevin was here. She did not know how important it was. All she knew is that she'd better listen.

She had not been lying when she said she respected the job. The FBI must have pulled some major strings and jumped through a lot of hoops to get Kevin in, and they weren't going to waste time and resources inserting someone into the MLB if they didn't have very good reason. She could put herself and who knew how many others at risk if she blew his cover. No, she would do what he needed from her whether or not she liked or even respected the man. The job he did was that important.

"Thank you," Kevin said.

Chapter Three

Lindsey was rather disappointed. That could have been an awesome article. Instead she stuck to the facts.

> *Kevin Baxter, the eye catching right fielder, swings the bat as well as he fields the ball. He went 6 for 10 this week with two home runs and a double. The Braves have got a great find in the modest Kevin Baxter. His brilliant defense and aggressive hitting will be warmly welcomed this season.*

This was only the first of Kevin's many write ups in the paper. He turned out to be a colossal player as the season rolled on. He was batting .390, and not many balls got past him in right field. He had a cannon of an arm. Lindsey had never seen anyone get the ball back to the infield like Kevin did. He was quickly making the cut off man look obsolete. He may not have wanted all the publicity, but he was definitely in the spot light now. Reporters all across the country were drawn to Kevin's magnificent talent.

The tremendous plays and outstanding at bats kept pumping out for Kevin Baxter. Lindsey found herself spending most of her time around Kevin. If she was not interviewing Kevin, she was interviewing someone around him. Kevin had become a very popular player not only with the fans but with the players as well.

Kevin was a hard worker. He was not vain. He was not strict or uptight. He treated others with the respect he expected in return. He was an overall good guy. People enjoyed being around Kevin, because he was such a fun person. Kevin always had a crowd of teammates around him, and for her job, Lindsey followed the crowd.

Lindsey never envisioned herself following Kevin around or spending so much time with him, but here she was. Kevin Baxter hardly resembled the FBI spokesperson who Lindsey had interviewed every week for years. He may have looked the same, but he had a whole new personality. Even if you had known him as both Brandon Cobb and Kevin Baxter as Lindsey did, you would swear they were two different people. Kevin Baxter was a genuinely happy person where as Brandon Cobb had been anything but.

Kevin Baxter was the complete opposite of Brandon Cobb. It was somewhat eerie, and Lindsey found herself wondering which personality was the man underneath.

Lindsey knew one thing for sure; he had a severe attitude adjustment since Forest Hills. Kevin Baxter was a very likable person.

After the Braves clinched another division title, which had finally become their MO again, Lindsey was invited to go to Kevin's house and celebrate with some of the players and their wives. Lindsey was sure that she would not have gotten the invite if not for Kevin.

He was trying to keep things between them friendly to say the least; he didn't want her ratting him out. This, nevertheless, was quite an honor and an exciting opportunity. The house was already crowded when Lindsey got there. Some of the players turned out to be nearly the entire team. Lindsey got interviews with everyone as the night flew by. The crowd slowly dwindled until Lindsey was the last one still there.

Lindsey sat down on the couch next to Kevin. "You're the only one here I haven't interviewed tonight. Are you avoiding me?" she wondered.

"I don't guess. Should I be?" Kevin responded.

"I don't see why. I've never written anything negative about you. You've had an amazing season."

"So have a lot of other guys. It takes more than one person to win a game. This ball club has been winning division titles years before I got here, and they'll still be winning division titles after I'm long gone," Kevin said modestly.

"I suppose you're right, but you've got to be proud of all you accomplished this season. Did you at least have fun?" Lindsey asked.

"Of course I had fun. I'm getting paid to play," Kevin answered.

"Can I ask you something off the record?"

"It's a free country. You can ask whatever you want, but I'm free too. I'll only answer what I want," Kevin replied.

"Did you really play in college or was that just part of your story?".

"Oh no. That was true. I played baseball the whole time I was growing up," Kevin answered.

"Did you miss it?" Lindsey asked.

"Yeah, I guess so. It's not that I have any regrets. I like my job when I'm not in trouble."

"Do you get in trouble a lot?"

"Give me a break. How many questions do you have? I know you didn't think I chose to be a spokesperson, and it was just my lucky day when I was assigned to Forest Hills. That was more or less a suspension," Kevin said with aggravation.

"I guess I never really thought about it."

"Ok, my turn to ask the questions. What are you doing here in Atlanta," Kevin asked.

"I'm following the team for the paper," Lindsey answered.

"Don't you find it strange that we both got reassigned to the same place close to the same time?"

"No, not really... Maybe a little... Ok, a lot. It totally freaked me out when I saw you that first day," Lindsey admitted.

"You think it freaked you out. I just knew my cover was blown. The name I made for myself playing ball in college was my last chance out of Forest Hills."

"What did you do to get in so much trouble?"

"I have no information on that at this time," Kevin responded with a smile.

Lindsey rolled her eyes. "I should have known," she teased.

"You better not turn out to be trouble. I didn't tell anyone about you knowing me. That's why I made sure you got invited tonight," Kevin said.

"You did that?" Lindsey asked feigning surprise.

"Umm-hmm," he mumbled.

"Why?"

"The closer you are the closer eye I can keep on you. If anyone finds out you knew me and I didn't say anything, I'll lose my job," Kevin said.

"Are you serious?"

"No. I find losing my job funny. Of course I'm serious," Kevin growled.

"Why didn't you say something then?" Lindsey asked.

"I didn't want to go back to Forest Hills. I would have been pulled real quick," Kevin replied.

"Why?"

"I told you that it was strange that we both got reassigned like that. The FBI has no way of proving that you aren't part of the problem," Kevin explained.

"Is it bad?" Lindsey asked.

"Is what bad?"

"Whatever you are here investigating," Lindsey clarified.

"I have no information on that at this time," Kevin responded except this time he wasn't smiling.

"You just said you thought I was in on it, and now you won't even tell me what it is," Lindsey argued.

"I didn't say that. I never said that. I'm taking a big chance assuming you're clean, and I don't bet everything I have on something I'm unsure about," Kevin nearly shouted.

Lindsey was stunned and silent for a few seconds. Ok, so that temper of his was real. "I am clean if that helps," she said.

"Thanks, but your word won't do me any good if I get caught," Kevin said calmly.

"I'm sorry."

"Don't be sorry. You didn't do anything. I put myself in this position. You just keep you mouth shut," Kevin instructed.

"I can do that," Lindsey agreed easily.

Chapter FOUR

Unfortunately, the Braves got eliminated after only the first series of the playoffs, but Lindsey had so much to tell Mr. Parks when she got home. Of course, she could not talk about who Kevin was, but he had done so much as far as the game itself was concerned that Lindsey could talk all off season long and still have more to tell. Lindsey and Mr. Parks talked constantly during the off season as usual.

It had been such an exciting year last season that Lindsey could not wait to get back to spring training. There was a new face in the bullpen, Nate Fields. He had been pulled up from Richmond. Of course, Nate Fields was not the only new face to the team, but he was the only new player already expected to make the starting lineup.

Lindsey got to the field early for the first practice of the season. Kevin and a couple of the other regulars were there for a little extra practice along with a small crowd of eager young players off a list of non-roster invitees. Lindsey interviewed with all the nervous young minor leaguers right up until practice started. After practice Lindsey caught up with Nate Fields and asked for an interview.

"I'm kind of busy right now, but maybe you could run by my hotel room later. Let's say about eight. I'm in room three-sixty-eight," he replied.

"It's not a problem. That will be great. I'll see you then," Lindsey said.

Being from a small town, it never occurred to Lindsey that meeting a stranger in his hotel room might not be a good idea. In Forest Hills it was not often that you met a stranger. Even then you did not have to worry much about whether anyone else was around or not. What harm could there be in a simple interview? What could happen?

Lindsey knocked on door three-sixty-eight. Nate opened the door. "You have perfect timing. Come on in," he said.

The room was beautiful and gigantic, much nicer than the rooms that she stayed in. Lindsey sat down on the couch. Nate sat down extremely close to her. He was almost sitting on top of Lindsey. Lindsey moved all the way to the end of the couch, but Nate followed her.

"Um, Mr. Fields," Lindsey started.

"Please, call me Nate," he interrupted.

"Ok well, let's get started then, Nate. What did you think about your first practice as a Brave?"

"I think it went well."

"There are some pretty steep expectations waiting for you back home in Atlanta. Do you feel you can fill all those expectations?" Lindsey asked.

"No problem. Are you seeing anyone, Lindsey?" Nate replied.

"I really don't know what that has to do with this interview, Nate," she responded.

"Of course, I'm sorry. Go on," he apologized.

"How do you see yourself living up to those expectations?"

"I don't foresee it being that hard. How did someone as pretty as you end up with this job anyway?"

"Nate, that's enough. I'm really not interested. Thank you. Could you tell me a little about your pitching?" Lindsey continued as if he had not been hitting on her at all. She was starting to realize that coming to his hotel room had been a mistake, a big mistake. How could she have been so stupid?

"I pitch everything hard and fast," he answered.

"Ok, do you have any specific pitches you concentrate more on?"

"How about this one," Nate said as he came towards her.

He tried to kiss her, but Lindsey pushed him back. "I'm really not interested, Nate. I would prefer if we stick to baseball, keep it professional," she told him.

"Professional? Right." Nate reached between two couch cushions and pulled out a pair of handcuffs. Lindsey tried to make a brake for the door, but Nate grabbed her and threw her back on the couch. Lindsey struggled to get free.

"What are you doing? Get off me," she squealed and fought back, but he was too strong. She could see now what she missed before. Nate's eyes were blood shot. He was on something. Whatever it was, it was stronger than just alcohol. He handcuffed her, then grabbed a scarf off the table and gagged her. Then there was a knock at the door.

"Just a minute," Nate called.

"One scream out of you and you'll only make it worse on yourself," he whispered.

Fat chance. Lindsey would rather take her chances that one of the other guys was out there. At least she did until Nate pulled a gun out of his pocket on his way to the door.

Nate opened the door part way and Lindsey heard Kevin's voice. "Have you seen Lindsey? A couple of the guys are looking for her," he said.

"Oh, yeah. She's in here. Come on in," Nate said opening the door all the way. Kevin walked in holding his fielding glove, and Nate hit him in the back of the head with the gun. Maybe he had been meaning to knock Kevin out, but it didn't work. Kevin dropped the glove and reached for his head.

"What the..." Kevin turned around and saw the gun pointed right at him.

"Get over there and sit down," Nate ordered. "Now gag yourself," he instructed. Once Kevin was gagged Nate pulled some more handcuffs out of a bag and cuffed Kevin too. A set of keys fell out of the bag as Nate pulled out the second pair of handcuffs, but he quickly scooped them up and dropped them into his pocket. Then Nate pulled out some rope and tied Kevin's feet together.

Nate sat down between Kevin and Lindsey. He sat the gun on the table and ran his hands down the front of Lindsey's blouse. Lindsey hated herself right now for wearing a V-neck, and she was seriously contemplating burning every V-neck she owned. More than that she hated herself for putting herself in this situation. The daughter of a cop, she should have known better.

There was another knock on the door. "Who is it?" Nate growled.

"You better get out here, man. There is a party going on, and we've got a drink downstairs with your name on it," a voice yelled.

Nate stood up and pointed the gun back and fourth between Lindsey and Kevin. "If anybody moves, somebody dies," he whispered. Then he put the gun in his pocket and left the room.

Kevin spit his gag out. He had obviously tied it loose. "Do you still want to know what I got in trouble for?" he asked.

Did he really expect her to answer? She was gagged for Pete's sake, and now is not the best time for small talk.

"I've got a real bad temper, and this guy is making me really angry. The next time he touches you, I want you to duck as far down as you can toward the other end of the couch," Kevin finished, and then he wiggled the scarf back into his mouth.

Lindsey did not know what Kevin was planning, but at this point she was ready to try anything. She only wished he would hurry up and get them out of here now while Nate was gone.

Nate was gone only a few minutes. When he got back, he came straight to the couch. He sat down and started sliding his hands up Lindsey's shirt. Lindsey did just as Kevin had instructed her. She jerked down as far as she could to the other end of the couch and buried her head. Lindsey heard a loud thud followed by another loud crash.

"Lindsey, get up and go get those keys," Kevin said.

When Lindsey got up, Nate was laying, out cold on the floor. Thank goodness that Kevin was more effective at knocking a person unconscious than Nate had been. She quickly got the keys and let Kevin out of the cuffs. Kevin untied his legs and undid Lindsey's handcuffs. Lindsey ungagged herself.

"Here put these on your friend down there," Kevin said handing Lindsey the handcuffs.

While Lindsey cuffed Nate, Kevin made a phone call. "I need discreet back up in room three-sixty-eight," he said.

Kevin tied Nate's legs together and to the handcuffs. "Have a seat. It won't take long," Kevin told her.

Lindsey did not ask what would not take long. She really did not want to know just as long as this whole nightmare was going to be over. In less than ten minutes the whole room was swarming with men. Lindsey stayed on the couch and did not move. Kevin huddled up in a corner of the room with two other men talking very quietly.

The last man to arrive was a big, tall man in a suit. He looked very mad, and he looked like he could seriously hurt someone if he wanted. He was a strong, buff man. He looked like the no nonsense type. The man shot an evil look in Lindsey's direction, and then started scanning the room. Lindsey did not know why he was mad at her, but she was not sticking around to find out.

She started easing her way across the room to Kevin.

"What's your problem?" Kevin asked. Then he looked up and saw the man. "Oh crap! What is he doing here? You owe me big time," Kevin said nudging Lindsey on the shoulder.

The man started towards them. Kevin met him only a few feet away from Lindsey.

"This is a fine mess you've made this time, kid. What were you doing here?" the man asked.

"I was returning his glove that got put in my bag by mistake," Kevin said.

The man glanced up at Lindsey. "What about the girl?"

"She won't be a problem. I can keep her quiet," Kevin replied.

"See to it that she isn't. I've never had to worry about you as far as women go. Tell me now if we've got a situation," the man said.

"My job comes first," Kevin responded, and the man nodded.

"I will not get called down here again. Is that understood?" the man asked.

"Yes, sir," Kevin answered.

"Good. Get her out of here so these men can do their job," the man said.

"Sanders, let's go," Kevin called.

She was back to a last name basis, but it didn't matter, not tonight. Lindsey quickly followed Kevin down the hall and into the emergency stairwell. As soon as he opened the door an alarm went off. Kevin shook his head. "You owe me a new glove. From now on do your interviews on the field," he said. That was all Kevin said. He walked Lindsey to her room, and then went his separate way.

Chapter Five

Needless to say, Lindsey did not get much sleep that night. She tossed and turned all night long. No matter what Lindsey did, she could not get to sleep. She was tense and fidgety. Her heart was racing, her head still pounding. She was scared to close her eyes. Lindsey was very aware of every bump in the night, and she was extremely jumpy. Each shadow on the wall seemed to dance around throughout the room. Fear plagued Lindsey's mind until early morning sunup. Sleep teased Lindsey, just out of reach, until the alarm sounded.

The next day at practice Lindsey was talking to the first and second basemen. "Hey, Lindsey, did you hear about the fire last night?" the second baseman asked.

"What fire?" Lindsey replied.

"There was a fire on the third floor of the hotel last night. Luckily, everyone was downstairs partying. Did you notice that new guy, Nate Fields, isn't here today? I heard that Fields was too scared to leave his room today," the second baseman added.

"That's not what I heard. I heard he was too hung over to come out," the first baseman interrupted.

"What are y'all flapping your gills about over here?" Kevin asked as he walked up.

"Hey, we were talking about Nate Fields. What did you hear?" the second baseman asked.

"A little bit of everything. Who cares? Drunk, hung over, or scared, if he can't get his butt to practice, he doesn't deserve to play," Kevin said.

"Yeah, you've got a point there," the first baseman agreed.

"Speaking of practice, we better get going," the second baseman said, and then he and the first baseman walked off.

Lindsey leaned in close to Kevin. "I was thinking… all night long actually. That wasn't a pitcher's glove you dropped last night," she said.

Kevin smiled slyly and said, "Let's put it this way. There were only three people in the room last night who know the difference, me, you, and Fields. It got you out of trouble without me losing my job. You better shut up and count your blessings when the good Lord hands them down."

"How did you know I was in trouble?" Lindsey asked.

"I told you. I'm keeping a close eye on you," Kevin replied.

"Did I ever say thank you?"

"I didn't hear anything to that effect."

"Thank you," Lindsey said gratefully.

"You're welcome," Kevin responded.

Lindsey was very grateful and found a new respect for Kevin that day. Any residual negative feelings she had from before were cleared away. It was almost as if Brandon Cobb had never existed. Kevin was getting a fresh start with a clean slate.

Everyone assumed that Nate Fields had quit when he did not show up for several days. By the end of the week word got around that he had mailed in his resignation. The team had a good laugh at all the wild rumors flying around, but by the end of spring training everyone had forgotten all about Nate Fields.

The season got off to a rocky start for the Braves, but somehow they managed to pull back ahead. Kevin's overwhelming success picked up right where he left off at the end of last season. He continued to swing a hot bat, and his defense was phenomenal. After their initial slump, the team as a whole delivered one well played game after another.

Before long, Lindsey was spending a lot more personal time with Kevin. They had quickly become friends. Lindsey would rather spend her time with the guys anyway. She saw them more than anyone else since she traveled with them. She knew them better and was more comfortable around them. They were only a couple of months into the season, and Lindsey had become one of the guys. She did everything with the team.

The season flew by. Before you could turn around, the Braves won another division title, but the victory was short lived. They got dropped out early in the race to the World Series. That was the story of their life. Every season it was the same thing. They would get off to a rocky start. Then they would pull through to win a division title, but never make it to the World Series.

Lindsey went home to Forest Hills for the off season, and as usual she talked Mr. Parks' ears off.

"Lindsey, what's the deal with Kevin Baxter? You talk about him constantly, dear. Everyday it's Kevin this and Kevin that. Is there something special about Kevin?" Mr. Parks asked.

"I don't know. He is a colossal player, but other than that, I don't guess so. Do I really talk about Kevin that much more than the others?" Lindsey asked.

"All the time, Lindsey, all the time," Mr. Parks told her with a knowing smile.

At spring training the next season, Lindsey was very careful not to make the same mistake twice. Any players that she did not previously know she interviewed in pairs. In the long run, interviewing in pairs worked out in everyone's favor. Lindsey was not putting herself into compromised situations, and the players were more comfortable. They really opened up quicker when they were not in the spotlight alone.

Spring training was getting off to a great start. Everyone was all smiles and playing great. This year's ball team was really something to see. All the players flowed together like a well oiled machine both on and off the field. Their personalities blended together to create a top notch baseball team destined, in Lindsey's opinion, for greatness.

Each position was played to the best of the player's ability, and the teamwork was really showing through. The teamwork paid off with the at bats as well. The Braves still had their share of home runs, but knocking it out of the park was not the main goal. The base hits were really adding up. The more men on base, the more came in. Get them on, get them over, and get them in. Now they were playing ABC ball. The Braves looked sensational this year. Lindsey could hardly wait for the start of the season.

The season started, and the Braves were not about to break from tradition. Once again, they started out in a slump. It did not take long to get rejuvenated, and the Braves were off and running again. Everything was perfect except one thing. Kevin was acting rather strange.

Lindsey knew that Kevin's job would have to be more stressful than the other players. His job involved an extensive amount more than just baseball. It did not seem out of the ordinary that Kevin should be more stressed, and it was taking its toll. At least it seemed that way to Lindsey, but Lindsey had concerns also.

This was the first time he acted so strange. He did not act this strange when everything happened with Nate Fields. How bad did things have to get before Kevin got stressed? That was a question Lindsey did not want an answer to. She had already seen more than enough FBI action to last her a lifetime. If whatever was bothering Kevin was worse than the Nate Fields incident, Lindsey wanted to have nothing to do with it. In fact, she did not want to be anywhere near when everything hit the fan. Lindsey started slowly distancing herself from Kevin.

The rest of the season seemed to drag by. The Braves were still playing wonderful ball, but Lindsey did not think she would ever make it home to Forest Hills. The Atlanta Braves won the division title again, and lost the first playoff series as usual. Lindsey had never been so glad to be wiped out so soon. She was finally going home.

As always Lindsey spent the off season with Mr. Parks. They talked about baseball from sun up till sun down. "Lindsey, is everything ok with Kevin Baxter?" Mr. Parks asked.

"Of course. He's a great player," Lindsey answered.

"Are you sure? Last year Kevin was all you talked about, but this year you hardly mention him," Mr. Parks noted.

"I still talk about Kevin. It's hard not to. You can't talk about the Braves success this year without mentioning Kevin Baxter. He's an unforgettable player," Lindsey explained.

"If you say so, Lindsey," Mr. Parks gave in, but he did so with what her mother used to call an "I know better" look.

Chapter Six

When spring training started up again Lindsey started dating one of the catchers, Aaron Diaz. He was a real sweet guy. He loved baseball. He was a Christian and super polite. He had been with the team for a year, and when he asked Lindsey out on the first day back to spring training, she couldn't resist saying yes.

For their first date he took her to The Melting Pot. Since Lindsey had never been, she wasn't sure what to expect, but she had a lot of fun laughing with Aaron.

The lighting was dim, perfect for romance, and Aaron was trying so hard. It must have killed the effect he was going for, though, when he had to look at Lindsey and admit that he didn't understand the menu.

"This is complicated. I don't know," he fessed up.

"I can understand. It's hard for me, and English is my first language. Maybe we should get the waiter to explain it," Lindsey suggested feeling sorry for Aaron.

The waiter had been willing and eager even to explain everything to them. As it turned out, a lot of people had trouble with figuring out how it all worked their first time.

The more Lindsey got to know Aaron over the course of the night the more she liked about him. He really was a well rounded guy. It appeared that he was as great a person off the field as he was on it. He was the precise kind of guy who Mr. Parks said made the best role models for young kids to look up to, and she loved him for it.

When Aaron and Lindsey went out, Aaron treated Lindsey like she was the most important thing in his life. Lindsey loved spending time with Aaron. They had fun together and always had a lot to talk about. Aaron was originally from Porto Rico, and when Aaron got excited or in too big a hurry he started spouting off in Spanish. Lindsey did not know much Spanish at all. She could count to ten, but not much more than that.

Lindsey did not know what to do when he started speaking Spanish to her. She would always throw her arms up in the air and say, "I have no idea what you're saying anymore." That would get Aaron laughing, and they would both have a real good laugh.

Aaron got traded before the end of spring training. Lindsey and Aaron promised to keep in touch and try at a long distance relationship. Aaron was traded to the Philadelphia Phillies, so it was not like they would only see one another once or twice a season. The Braves and the Phillies were in the same division, so they would play each other quite a bit during a season.

Avoiding Kevin this season was easier than ever. In fact, it looked very much like Kevin was the one avoiding Lindsey this season. In fact, Lindsey had a hard time tracking Kevin down for interviews.

If she could find Kevin, he always kept it short and had somewhere else to be. Kevin had never been so hard to get an interview with. The other guys were all comfortable with Lindsey and more than accommodating. Lindsey did more interviews with the other players to make up for what she was missing with Kevin.

Lindsey may have had trouble getting an interview, but the Braves were having no trouble playing. Their defense was awesome. Their pitching was dynamic. Even their at bats were looking good. Everything was flowing right along for the Braves. Nothing could get in their way now. That seemed to be the case anyway until Kevin Baxter's batting hit a slump.

He quit making contact with the ball, and his batting average started to decline rapidly. His slump brought down the whole team's spirits.

Although Kevin's batting average was suffering, he still made the all-star team. The all-star team is partly a popularity contest, and Kevin Baxter was a very popular player. He was popular with both the fans and the other players. Several other Braves members made the all-star team as well.

Lindsey worked hard to get an interview with everyone on the National League all-star team. Some players were more cooperative than others. Most of them did not know Lindsey as well as the Braves players did, so getting an interview with them was a little tricky.

Kevin could never be found, however. He was always long gone by the time Lindsey could get there. She tried over and over to get an interview with Kevin, but it just was not going to happen.

Lindsey and Aaron went out to a club with a good many of the other players the night before the all-star game. It was not necessarily Lindsey's idea. She was not real big on the idea of late nights before a game. Not to mention a fair majority of the players would be drinking heavily tonight.

If they got trashed, they were going to have a hang over the next day. Now, Lindsey did not care what they did. It was their own business. If they did not mind the hang over and other consequences, that was fine, but they needed to do it on their own time. A lot of people watch the all-star game, and now a lot of people were counting on that all-star game for home field advantage in the World Series. With so much responsibility resting on their shoulders, tomorrow was not the day to be hung over.

Lindsey's opinion did not amount to much. There were men already drunk when Aaron and Lindsey got there. Man, some of them got crazy when they were drunk. The whole night was a laugh riot. Lindsey had a ball watching everyone else. Aaron was not a big drinker. He had a couple of beers all night long. Lindsey ordered a strawberry daiquiri that she sipped on but never finished. Aaron and Lindsey danced and laughed.

Aaron loved to dance and have a good time just being silly. The first time he had ever drug Lindsey out on a dance floor she thought that she would die of embarrassment. She didn't know how to dance, but she quickly learned that neither did Aaron. He was out there just to have a good time despite what anyone else thought. They were having a good time until Kevin brought the night to a screeching halt.

Kevin was on the other end of the room and getting very loud. This was odd for Kevin. He normally did not draw a lot of attention to himself, and Lindsey had never seen him get drunk. He always limited himself before. One thing was for sure. He was causing a scene now and looked to be out of control.

"What's wrong with Kevin? He looks mad at someone," Aaron observed.

"Yeah, he does," Lindsey agreed.

"He doesn't get mad easy. Do you think he's ok?" Aaron asked.

Now Lindsey knew better than that. Kevin did get mad easy. He had a volatile temper, but he tried not to let it show in public. It did not take much to get him started. You would definitely know when Kevin was mad, but he did not usually make such a spectacle of himself. He would handle whatever problem he had with that person, not the whole room.

"I don't know what's bothering him. I haven't talked to him much lately," Lindsey replied.

Kevin threw a bottle against a wall, and the Braves short stop started pushing his way through the crowd towards Lindsey and Aaron. "Lindsey, would you talk to him? See if you can calm him down. No one knows what he's griping about," the short stop said.

"Why me?" Lindsey asked.

"No one can understand what he's talking about, but we've heard your name very distinctively a couple of times," the short stop replied. Aaron did not look like he liked the idea at all. "We won't let him hurt Lindsey. If somebody doesn't do something soon, Kevin is going to spend the all-star game in jail. The bartender is getting aggravated with him," the short stop explained.

"How much has he had to drink?" Lindsey asked.

"Who knows? I don't think anyone could keep up with him tonight," the short stop answered.

"Kevin never drinks that much. Didn't anyone find it strange before he got to this point?" Lindsey demanded.

"He's a grown man, Lindsey. Besides Kevin has been in a mood all night," the short stop said.

With a sigh, Lindsey got up and started in Kevin's direction, but before she could get more than a step away, Aaron grabbed her arm. "Lindsey, you can't be serious. You can't go over there," he said.

She was serious, though, very serious. Kevin was out of control and violent. There was a chance that she could calm him down. If Lindsey did not try and someone got hurt, she would never forgive herself.

"The Braves need him at the plate not behind bars. I'm just going to see if he'll talk to me. If he won't then I'll come straight back," Lindsey said.

"I don't like this. I'm not going over there," Aaron insisted.

"Fine. You stay here, and I'll be right back."

"Lindsey wait," Aaron called, but it was too late. Lindsey was already gone.

Kevin did not see Lindsey when she first got over there. The short stop was right. You could not understand one single word Kevin was saying. His speech was not slurred, but he was screaming so fast that it was impossible to keep up.

"Kevin?" Lindsey called.

Kevin spun around. "What do you want?" he growled.

"I just came to see if you are ok," Lindsey replied.

"You can see I'm just fine."

"I can see you're drunk."

"Yup. Are you going to write it up?" Kevin asked.

"No, but I thought you didn't drink before a game."

"I do tonight. Is it any of your business?"

"Maybe not, but the cops will make it their business," Lindsey answered.

"Is that supposed to scare me? Local PD aren't a threat," Kevin said starting to scream again. Then he threw another bottle against the wall.

"That's it! One of you get him out of here now or I'll have him escorted out," the bartender shouted.

A couple of guys tried to lead Kevin toward the door, but he pushed them off.

"Kevin, they're trying to help," Lindsey said.

"I don't need any help," Kevin told her.

"Then do it on your own, but you still have to leave," Lindsey said.

"I'll leave when I get ready," Kevin shouted. He grabbed his stomach and groaned.

"You're going to be sick," Lindsey noted.

"I don't care," Kevin grumbled, and then grabbed his stomach again.

"Come on. Let's get out of here. I'll help this time," Lindsey offered.

Kevin allowed Lindsey to guide him to the door. He could hardly walk on his own. Lindsey was having a hard time keeping both herself and Kevin on their feet. Kevin was nearly pulling her down with him. They barely made it out of the doorway before Kevin got sick. Lindsey waited with Kevin until he stopped vomiting.

"The hotel is two blocks away. So, you think you can make it that far?" Lindsey asked.

Kevin nodded.

"Good. Let's get you to your room."

Kevin was barely dragging himself along, with help of course. "I don't feel so good," he said.

"I don't guess so. How much did you drink tonight?" Lindsey asked.

Kevin shrugged his shoulders and started throwing up again. When they got to Kevin's hotel room, he fell in the doorway.

"Kevin, please, don't pass out on me now. You're so close to the bed," Lindsey mumbled.

She tried to drag Kevin inside so that she could shut the door, but it was no use. Suddenly Kevin jerked up and started crawling as quickly as he could toward the bathroom. Lindsey shut the door and went after Kevin who was hugging the toilet in the dark. Lindsey flipped the light on but quickly turned it off again when Kevin started groaning.

Lindsey wet a rag and sat down in the floor next to Kevin. Kevin pulled his head out of the toilet and looked at Lindsey. "What are you doing still here?" he asked.

"I can't leave you like this," Lindsey answered and started wiping his face with the rag. "Kevin, what happened?"

"I drank too much," he slurred.

"Well, I can see that. Why did you drink so much?"

"I just felt like it. What's with the third degree? I should have taken my chances with the police," Kevin said.

"What is your problem?" Lindsey snapped.

"You," Kevin shot back.

"Me? I haven't done anything to you."

"You don't know what you've done to me," Kevin shouted.

"Ok. Fine. Have it your way. All this is my fault. What did I do that was so horrible?"

"Everything," Kevin propped his head up on the toilet. "Nothing, I guess. I don't know. I never had this problem before. I was focused," he said as he started to doze off.

"Kevin, wake up. Let's get you to bed before you pass out," Lindsey said.

Kevin mumbled under his breath while Lindsey helped drag him to bed. He was mumbling something about his problem and his job. He clearly was not making sense anymore. Lindsey helped him into bed and covered him up.

"I love you," Kevin whispered.

"Ok. Shhhh. Go to sleep, Kevin," Lindsey said softly. By this point Lindsey was not paying any attention to what he said. He was out of it. Lindsey found some aspirin on the bathroom counter. She got a glass of water and set it out on the night stand with two aspirins. Then, she left out to go find Aaron.

She did not have to go far to find Aaron. He met her in the hall. "Is everything ok?" he asked.

"Yeah, Kevin is seriously messed up though. He may not be any good for tomorrow's game. I laid out some aspirin, but he's going to have a major hang over," Lindsey said.

"You can't help that. Kevin is Kevin's responsibility, not yours," Aaron told her. Aaron and Lindsey decided to call it a night and both turned in.

At six the next morning Lindsey was awakened by a knock at the door. Who in the world would be knocking at the door at six in the morning? It was still early. Lindsey opened the door. "Kevin?" she said.

Kevin winced in pain. He was holding his head and was obviously hung over bad.

"What do you want?" Lindsey whispered.

"I wanted to apologize. I haven't drunk like that in years. I don't remember much about last night, so if I said or did anything inappropriate, I'm sorry," Kevin suffered to get out.

"Don't worry about it. I learned a long time ago not to take people serious when they are that drunk," Lindsey said.

"Thanks," Kevin replied. He started to leave.

"Hey, I think I earned an interview last night," Lindsey called after him.

Kevin tried to smile. "I'll keep that in mind," he said.

Kevin was definitely not at the top of his game that day, and he did not stay in the game long. Despite Kevin's despairing efforts the rest of the national league all-star team played their hearts out. The national league came out on top with a ten to eight victory.

Lindsey caught up with Kevin when they got back to Atlanta. "How about that interview?" she asked.

Kevin nodded his head. "What do you want to know?"

"Anything you'll tell me. What about your batting? What's happened?" Lindsey asked.

"I hit a slump," Kevin answered.

"That's it? You hit a slump. You have no idea what's going on?" Lindsey asked.

"If I knew what was going on then I could fix it. Couldn't I? I'm just not seeing the ball. I'm not focused or something. Listen, I've got to go. We can finish this later," Kevin said.

Well, so much for that interview. Why was he being so evasive?

Chapter Seven

They did finish the interview later, much to Lindsey's relief. After that Kevin was not so hard to track down for interviews. He was readily accessible for interviewing, but he would split as soon as they finished. Lindsey and Kevin never talked anymore other than interview situations.

It was strange how they had come full circle. When she had been reporting FBI updates, they hadn't gotten along at all. After a while of working together through baseball, they had actually become good friends. Now they were more like acquaintances, but Lindsey tried not to give it much thought. Kevin had other things on his mind. He was busy, and whatever was going on, Lindsey did not want to get in the way.

Aaron started getting jealous. "Why do you have to do so many interviews with Kevin all of the sudden?" he asked.

"It's my job, Aaron."

"Then quit," Aaron popped off.

"Aaron can you hear yourself? I need my job to pay bills, and it just so happens that I like my job."

"Well, I don't," Aaron responded.

"Well, that's just too bad then. Isn't it? What has gotten into you lately?" Lindsey asked.

The answer came back in Spanish. Lindsey just shook her head and let him ramble on. She could not speak a word of Spanish so there was no sense in trying to follow what he was saying. Maybe having a chance to get things off his chest in his own language would calm him down.

Aaron went on for at least five minutes straight. The only word Lindsey ever picked up on was Julio. Julio is Aaron's best friend. He was from Puerto Rico where they grew up together. Lindsey knew things had been rocky between them for a while now. Aaron had been complaining about Julio for two and a half months now. They had not really been fighting or anything. Aaron said that Julio had picked up an attitude in the last year or so.

Lindsey had met Julio a couple of times, and she agreed fully. Julio had a big attitude problem. He really did not like Lindsey, but Lindsey had done nothing to make Julio hate her so. Aaron insisted that she and Julio had just gotten off to a rough start. Maybe they met when Julio was having a bad day or something, but Lindsey was not so sure. Julio seemed to really hate her, and she was not the only one that Julio disliked so passionately. To be honest, Julio didn't appear to like anyone.

Lindsey even thought she was beginning to notice a pattern. Julio did not seem to like anyone who was American born especially. He still didn't like others, but his hate for Americans just seemed to go a little deeper. Lindsey never said anything to Aaron. She was almost positive that she was imagining the whole thing. She had to be. That was ridiculous. Aaron would have noticed it by now surely. Lindsey must be over reacting, but there was definitely something wrong whatever it was. Now Julio kept brushing Aaron off. Aaron said that he had just fallen in with the wrong crowd.

"Hold up. What do I have to do with Julio?" Lindsey interrupted Aaron's Spanish tirade.

"Nothing. Julio is too far gone. Just forget Julio," Aaron snapped.

"You're the one who brought him up not me," Lindsey reminded him.

"This is stupid. You're going to have to choose me or Kevin," Aaron demanded.

"Aaron you're being ridiculous. There is nothing going on with Kevin. It's just my job," Lindsey insisted.

"Your job then. What's it going to be, me or your job?"

"You're giving me an ultimatum?" Lindsey asked stunned.

"What? I don't know. I'm telling you to choose me or your job," Aaron repeated.

"Aaron, don't do this," Lindsey begged.

"Why not? Are you choosing your job?"

"I don't want to be with someone who is making me chose like this. Aaron, this is silly," Lindsey argued.

"No, Lindsey, we are silly. Maybe this is the end of us," Aaron said.

Lindsey did not know what to say. She stood there and watched Aaron walk away. She did not try to stop him. She did not call after him. She stood frozen and watched. It felt sort of like a betrayal. Why would he make her choose like that? She stood there waiting. If she waited long enough, surely he would come back and tell her it was all a mistake and that he didn't mean it.

It did not take long for news of the break up to get around. Lindsey could not get Aaron off her mind and everywhere she turned someone else was talking about him. Lindsey and Aaron were so close to just lose it all like that.

Well, they had not been dating all that long, she supposed, but they had just clicked together so well. They were comfortable with one another. They knew how to make each other laugh. They could always count on each other. Aaron was sweet and kind. He was strong and secure yet gentle at the same time.

Lindsey loved Aaron. She loved everything about him. She loved his sense of humor. She loved his serious side. She loved his silly side. She loved his dedication. She loved his hair, his lips, his smile, his skin, and his eyes. She loved his accent. She even loved when he started speaking Spanish without noticing. Lindsey still loved Aaron very, very much.

She moped around the remainder of the season. She heard that Aaron was not taking things well either, but that was not apparent in his game. Both his defense and his offence took off after the brake up.

The off season got off to a slow start. Lindsey did not feel like talking about baseball, and Mr. Parks did not push her.

In mid December Aaron showed up in Forest Hills with flowers. "I'm sorry, Lindsey. I may have over reacted. I've been upset about Julio, and I guess I took that out on you. If you say there is nothing going on with Kevin, then there is nothing going on. I have no reason not to trust you. Can we try again?"

"I don't know Aaron. I shouldn't have to choose," Lindsey said.

"No, you shouldn't. I was wrong to ask that," Aaron agreed.

"Well, ok, but if things get weird again..."

"No, they won't. I promise, Lindsey," Aaron said cutting her off. Lindsey really did want to try again more than anything, but the fact remained that it did happen. Lindsey still felt very strong about not having to choose. There was absolutely nothing between her and Kevin. She should not have to prove that. Kevin was just a friend. Aaron would have to trust her. If he could not trust her, then things could never work out.

Lindsey and Aaron tried to pick up right where they left off, but by late January Julio was all Aaron talked about. "I think he's in real trouble. He's hanging around a bad group. I don't know where they are from or what they do. They look real dangerous. I have a real bad feeling about them, but Julio won't listen. He doesn't want anything to do with me anymore. He told me to stay away. I talked with Mama last week. No one back home has heard from him in a long time. That isn't like Julio. Something bad is going on with him," Aaron said.

Lindsey did not know Julio all that well, but Aaron worried about him constantly.

Spring training started up again. Aaron and Lindsey worked all season long to put things back together. Things never did go back to normal for them. Things were different. Things between them weren't so much strained but stiff, maybe. They were too platonic. They were still close, but they lacked the intimacy to the relationship that they had before. They tried hard, but in the end they were good friends and nothing more. Lindsey still loved Aaron, and Aaron still loved Lindsey. They still looked out for each other and would do anything for one another, but it just was not the same.

Chapter EIGHT

The Braves were having a picture perfect season. "Would you say things are progressing out of your previous slump?" Lindsey asked during an interview with Kevin.

"I don't know. What would you say?" he replied.

"The reporter isn't supposed to answer her own questions," Lindsey told him.

"Off the record," Kevin said.

"Off the record," Lindsey repeated with a laugh.

"Yeah, off the record. How do you think I'm doing behind the plate?"

"Average," Lindsey answered.

"Average isn't bad," Kevin sighed.

"It is for you. You're not an average player."

"Is that so? What am I doing wrong? Um, I've got to go," Kevin said suddenly.

"Now?" Lindsey asked.

"Yeah, sorry."

"But you didn't answer anything," Lindsey protested.

"Later. I promise," Kevin said.

"When?"

"Your call."

Kevin was always running out like that. Lindsey had gotten long, sit down interviews with everyone about this season, everyone except Kevin. Lindsey was determined to interview Kevin. She didn't think he was doing it on purpose. He just kept running off like he had somewhere he had to be. He was always so busy, but tomorrow was another day. Tomorrow was an off day, so Lindsey made plans to swing by Kevin's house around three o'clock unannounced.

Kevin looked surprised when he opened the door. "Lindsey, what are you doing here?" he asked.

"You promised me an interview," she answered.

"Yeah, um... I did promise. I'll do it too, but now isn't a good time," Kevin said.

"You said it was my call," Lindsey reminded him.

"I know I did, Lindsey, but now really isn't going to work," Kevin insisted. There was no chance that Lindsey was going to let Kevin out that easy. She wanted this interview done today while they had an off day. What to do about it though. It wasn't as if she could make him answer her questions.

"Of course not. I should have known," Lindsey responded both disappointed and aggravated.

"Come on now. Don't do that."

"Don't do what?"

"Don't act like that. I don't always let you down," he replied.

"Are you sure?"

"Am I sure? What is that supposed to mean?" Kevin wanted to know.

"I wanted to get a sit down interview with the whole team on this season's success. I finished everyone else's a week or more ago. You're always too busy," Lindsey explained.

"Oh, Lindsey, you understand. Don't you? I'm... You are important. It's just that... I can't... Oh, come on," Kevin said opening the door for Lindsey.

"You mean it?" she asked.

"Yes. Hurry before I change my mind," Kevin said.

Lindsey walked in and followed Kevin to the living room. When they got to the living room, stuff was set up everywhere. There was a computer and printer. There was a speaker talking in another language that Lindsey did not recognize. Wires were running everywhere. The floor was covered in huge stacks of paper. "What's all this?" Lindsey asked.

"I have no information on that at this time. Look, you're the one who wanted to do this right now. You see nothing. You hear nothing. Understood?" Kevin instructed.

Lindsey nodded. "Why didn't you say something?" she asked.

"I tried. We were standing out in the open. What did you want me to say? *Not now, Lindsey. I'm busy with spy work.*"

"Something like that. Yeah," Lindsey replied. Great job, Lindsey, she thought ruthlessly. He tried to tell you he couldn't do it right now, but no, you had to go and force his hand.

"Go ahead with your interview. Pretend none of it's here," Kevin told her.

Lindsey tried, but it was easier said than done. Sitting in the middle of everything was nerve racking.

"I don't know if I can do this. All this is a little too real," Lindsey admitted.

"Sure you can. You knew that I worked for the FBI. It was always real. What changed?" Kevin asked.

"I don't know. Nothing really changed. It was easier to ignore what I couldn't see," Lindsey explained.

"Oh, as long as you couldn't see any evidence of it, you didn't have to believe it, huh? Why are you so scared?" Kevin asked.

"I didn't say I was scared," Lindsey replied.

"You didn't have to. What are you so scared of?" Kevin asked.

"You remember Nate Fields. I hated that. That scared me. I have never been so scared. I don't want to relive that," Lindsey admitted.

"You got yourself into that situation. It had nothing to do with me. If it had been anyone else in that room with him, I wouldn't have touched him with a ten foot pole. He was local PD's problem, not mine. Causing a scene is not a good idea in this business. If you don't put yourself in that position, you won't have to live through it again, but... if you do end up in that position again you won't have to go through it alone. I'll be there for you, so try not to worry about it as much. I can't seem to let you go. Look, don't worry about any of this; just do your interview," Kevin said.

Lindsey looked around the room trying to catch her breath and convince herself that everything was ok. "What were you saying about my hitting yesterday?" Kevin asked.

"What?" Lindsey responded.

"Something about average not being good enough," Kevin reminded her.

"Oh, yeah. You're not hitting like you should be," Lindsey said.

"What's wrong with the way I'm hitting?" Kevin asked.

"Well, it looks like your head is somewhere else. It's like you're distracted. I can see why now," Lindsey answered. Lindsey started to leave. "I shouldn't be here while you're trying to work. We can do this another time," she said.

Kevin grabbed her hand to stop her. "Wait. You're fine. You're not hurting a thing. All this stuff really isn't what has been distracting me lately anyway," he said.

"It' not?"

"Nope," Kevin answered.

"It's distracting me," Lindsey responded.

"I can see that. Come, sit down, and let me interrogate you for a while until you get used to it," Kevin suggested.

"Interrogate?" Lindsey asked.

"Yeah. I interrogate. I don't interview," Kevin explained.

"Oh," Lindsey mumbled.

"What's the deal with you and Aaron?"

"The deal?" Lindsey repeated.

"Are you still together?"

"We're friends," Lindsey answered. Kevin visibly relaxed after that answer.

"How well do you know Julio Sosa?"

"He's Aaron's best friend."

"I want you to stay away from him," Kevin warned.

"He's in trouble. Isn't he?"

"What makes you think he's in trouble?" Kevin asked.

"Aaron thinks he's in trouble."

"Why does Aaron think that?"

"He said Julio fell in with the wrong crowd," Lindsey explained.

"What kind of crowd?"

"I don't know," Lindsey replied.

"Have you ever met this crowd?"

"No," Lindsey responded.

"What did Aaron say about the crowd?".

"He said they were trouble and that they looked dangerous," Lindsey told him.

"Aaron has met this group?" Kevin asked.

"Once or twice."

"Does Aaron still hang out with Julio a good bit?" Kevin asked.

"No, Julio won't have anything to do with him," Lindsey replied.

"Your turn," Kevin turned the conversation.

"Why can't you focus at the plate?" Lindsey asked.

"My mind is on other things," Kevin admitted.

"On all this?" Lindsey asked looking around.

"No," Kevin responded.

"On Julio?" Lindsey asked.

"No."

"I don't get it. Where is your mind when you go up to bat?" Lindsey asked.

"Thinking about things I shouldn't be, I'm sure," Kevin replied.

"Like what?" Lindsey asked.

"Like you," Kevin answered.

Lindsey did not stop to think before she spoke. If Lindsey had stopped to think for just one minute she would have noticed the look in Kevin's eyes. A look that maybe she had never noticed before. Was it a look of concern or maybe more?

"Me? What did I do?" she asked.

"I wish I knew," Kevin responded.

"Why are you thinking about me?"

"I don't know that either."

Before the conversation could go any further the speaker on the coffee table shifted languages and caught Lindsey's attention. "That's Spanish. That thing wasn't playing Spanish when I came in," she said.

"No it wasn't. It really doesn't matter what language they start speaking. The computer is translating it and printing it out as they go," Kevin explained. Another voice started also speaking Spanish.

"That's Aaron," Lindsey said.

"I don't know," Kevin replied.

"I'm telling you that is Aaron. I know his voice. That is Aaron. What is that thing?" Lindsey demanded.

"I have no information on that at this time," Kevin responded with a playful smile, but Lindsey was feeling anything but playful.

"Stop it, Kevin. Why is Aaron's voice playing on that little speaker?" she asked again.

"I can't tell you that," Kevin told her.

"Well, what is it? What is it playing? When was that? Who is he talking to?" Lindsey asked.

"I can't answer any of that. I thought you wanted to talk about baseball," Kevin lead.

"Don't change the subject. Is Aaron in trouble?" Lindsey asked.

"I don't think so," Kevin replied.

"Why is he on that?"

"I can't answer that, and even if I could, right now I really don't know."

"What can you answer?" Lindsey asked.

"You already know what I can and can't answer," Kevin said.

"Just tell me one thing. Is Aaron in danger?" Lindsey asked.

"I don't know," Kevin answered honestly.

"I have to find him. Where is he?" Lindsey asked.

"Lindsey, I can't..." Kevin started.

"Don't say it, Kevin. If he's in danger I have to find him. Where is he?"

"I can't tell you that. Doesn't he have a phone or someway you can get in touch with him?" Kevin asked.

"Yes," Lindsey answered.

"Ok. Call him, but remember you can't tell him anything. We've got to go to another room or he'll hear the echo from the speaker," Kevin said.

Lindsey followed Kevin to the kitchen then called Aaron.

"Hello," Aaron answered.

"Hey," Lindsey responded.

"Lindsey, this really isn't a good time. Can I call you back?"

"Is everything ok? You're worrying me," Lindsey said. Kevin shot her a stern look over the counter.

"Everything is fine. Why are you worried?" Aaron asked.

"You don't sound like yourself. What are you doing?"

"I'm trying to talk with Julio. Let me call you later," Aaron said.

"Wait. Aaron. Where are you?" Lindsey asked.

"I'm at Julio's. What is wrong with you?" Aaron asked.

"Nothing. It just scares me, that's all," Lindsey replied. Kevin shot her another warning look.

"What does? Lindsey, are you ok?" Aaron asked.

"Yes, I'm fine. I just wish you wouldn't go over to Julio's anymore," Lindsey answered.

"Why?" Aaron asked.

"Those people Julio has been hanging out with. You said they look dangerous. I worry about you when you go over there. Do you have to go over there?" Lindsey asked.

"He's my best friend, Lindsey. Don't be ridiculous," Aaron said.

"I know he is, but Aaron, you don't know much about his new friends. What you do know, you don't like. Can't you meet him somewhere more public?" Lindsey asked.

"Stop. Nothing is going to happen. You're worrying about nothing. Julio is my best friend. Now, I really have to go. Good-bye, Lindsey," Aaron said and hung up. "No, wait," Lindsey shouted into the phone, but she was too late. Aaron was gone.

"I have to call him back," Lindsey said franticly.

"No, you don't," Kevin said. He tried to take the phone from her, but she squirmed away too quickly. Lindsey was sent directly to Aaron's voice mail.

"He turned it off," Lindsey cried.

"Good," Kevin said.

Lindsey ran back to the living room. The people on the speaker were not speaking Spanish any longer, and Lindsey did not recognize the language being spoken.

"What... What is that?" Lindsey asked, but Kevin did not answer.

Lindsey heard Aaron's voice in Spanish again followed by someone else speaking Spanish. The second person started shouting. Then Aaron started, and they were both shouting.

"What's going on? Who is that? Is that Julio? Why is he yelling? What are they saying?" Lindsey asked in a panic, but Kevin did not say a word.

Lindsey listened as the two men on the speaker continued shouting. The shouting got louder and harsher. It seemed to go on for an eternity. Lindsey was frightened and did not think it would ever end. She jumped when she heard a loud bang from the speaker. Tears started quickly streaking down her face.

"What was that?" Lindsey asked slowly.

"It sounded like a door slamming to me," Kevin replied.

"A door?" Lindsey repeated.

"Yes. What did you think?"

Lindsey carefully sat down on the couch. "It was just a door?" she asked.

"I could be wrong, but that is what it sounded like," Kevin said.

"It wasn't a gun?" Lindsey asked.

"Good grief, no. It wasn't loud enough to be a gun shot. I can double check the print out, but I really think it was a door," he said.

Kevin walked over to the printer and pulled out a small stack of papers. He looked over the papers a few minutes then said, "Yeah. It was a door slamming. Aaron left. Everything is ok. Why don't I drive you home now?"

"No. That's ok," Lindsey responded.

"You're in no condition to drive, and I don't think we'll finish the interview today," Kevin said.

Lindsey reluctantly gave in, and Kevin drove her home. She did not talk to Aaron again until early the next morning. By then Lindsey was much calmer.

"I'm sorry I forgot to call back last night. I got into an argument with Julio. I was upset and just forgot. I'm sorry, Lindsey," Aaron apologized.

"Oh, it's alright. Is everything ok now?" Lindsey asked.

"No. I don't think so. Not this time, Lindsey. These are some real bad men," Aaron said.

"What do they do that is so bad?" Lindsey asked.

"I don't know, but I'm sure it's not legal. It looks really big time too. I can't understand what they are talking about. I can't speak their language, but Julio has learned to. It's almost like he's brain washed or something. They think for him now.

"I don't know him anymore. He's not the Julio I grew up with. I have a bad feeling that he's going to get himself killed. I've tried to talk to him, but he won't listen. He doesn't want anything to do with me if I won't join his new friends.

"Lindsey, what was I supposed to do? I can't join them. I don't know who they are, what they do, or what they believe in. I know I don't trust them. I can't join a group like that. The Julio I knew wouldn't either. I don't know what's gotten into him.

"He said that if I wasn't with them, then I was against them. How could he say that? We've been there for each other through everything. We've always been able to depend on each other. I would do anything for him, but I don't think this new group is good for him.

"I'm so worried about him. I don't want to visit him in jail. What will I tell his mother? Who will tell his father? His father would be so disappointed. All Julio's brothers look up to him. What will they be told? Lindsey, what should I do?" Aaron asked.

"I don't know that there is anything you can do, Aaron. Julio is a grown man. You can't choose his friends for him. All we can do now is pray," Lindsey replied.

Aaron was very upset. It was obvious that he needed someone to talk to. He needed someone to listen while he got it all off his chest. Plus, Lindsey thought she could take any information that Aaron dropped back to Kevin and help keep Aaron safe.

"I know, Lindsey, and I do. I pray for him every chance I get, but is it enough? He is my best friend. I feel sort of responsible for him. I want to do more, but he makes it so impossible. He said that I was the enemy now and to get out of his house." Aaron switched over to Spanish. He talked for another thirty minutes in Spanish.

Lindsey could not understand him, but that did not matter much right now. Aaron needed her. If he needed to speak Spanish, then that is what she would listen to. She certainly would not want to try to speak another language when she was upset. It is not right that Aaron should have to either. For right now, all she could do was let him vent.

Aaron sighed. "Lindsey, how long have I been speaking Spanish?" he asked.

"A while."

"Why did you not stop me?"

"You were upset. Spanish is comfortable to you. I didn't want to stop you," Lindsey explained.

"Thank you, but you can't understand a word of Spanish," Aaron reminded her.

"I know, but I can still listen," Lindsey replied.

"How would you like me to teach you some Spanish?" Aaron asked.

"Really?" Lindsey responded.

"Sure. I've got to get to the ball park right now, but we'll set up a time later," Aaron said. Lindsey was excited about learning Spanish. She'd be able to communicate with the guys so much better.

Lindsey wanted to tell Kevin everything Aaron had told her, so she caught up with Kevin after the game. "I need to talk to you," Lindsey said.

"Can't it wait?" Kevin asked.

"No," she responded.

"Well, I'm going to get something to eat. You can join me if you want," Kevin offered. Lindsey waited until they were alone in Kevin's truck.

"I talked to Aaron this morning. He said that Julio told him that if he wasn't on their side then he was against them. Julio called Aaron his enemy. Aaron said Julio learned to speak his new friends' language, and he said that it was like Julio was brain washed," Lindsey said. She wanted to get everything out as quickly as she could. It had to be important.

"Whoa, slow down. I've got their argument on tape remember. I've already read every word," Kevin said.

"Kevin, what's going on? Please, I have to know."

"You know that I can't tell you that," Kevin reminded her.

"Please, I need to know that Aaron is safe," Lindsey pleaded.

"Aaron will be just fine as long as he keeps his distance from Julio and his new friends," Kevin assured her.

"How can he? The Phillies start a four game series with the Mets next week. Julio plays for the Mets," Lindsey noted.

"I'm fully aware of where Julio plays. I know the Mets are in Philadelphia next week, but I think Aaron is ok. As long as Aaron doesn't pose a threat to this group, they have bigger fish to fry," Kevin explained.

"How could Aaron pose a threat to them?"

"Well, if he knew who they were or what they are doing, he could be a very real threat to them. If he threatened to expose them, he would not have lived this long," Kevin answered.

"Oh," Lindsey gasped.

"Relax. You said Aaron doesn't know anything. Right? He just has a bad feeling about them. Right?"

"Yes."

"Aaron doesn't pose any threat at all to them," Kevin assured her.

Chapter Nine

The Braves and Phillies did not see each other again for almost two weeks. The Braves had a series at home with the Nationals, and then went to Miami to play the Marlins in a three game series. Next, they came home to meet the Diamondbacks followed by the Phillies.

The Phillies had a couple of series out west with the Dodgers and the Giants. Then they came home to play the Mets followed by a road trip to Atlanta.

The Phillies and Braves would have an off day between the first and second games of their series together. Lindsey and Aaron made plans to spend the day together. Aaron was going to give Lindsey her first Spanish lesson that day.

The Braves swept both the Marlins and the Diamondbacks. They took two out of three with the Nationals. After the Diamondbacks series, a bunch of the guys went out to get a bite to eat, and Lindsey tagged along.

They could not go anywhere without Lindsey these days. Since Lindsey could not be close to Aaron and know that he was safe, she did the next best thing. Lindsey stuck to Kevin like glue. She thought Kevin would know if something was wrong with Aaron and Julio.

As they walked into the restaurant, there was a crowd around every TV. Someone who recognized one of the players yelled out, "Hey. Get over here, man. You've got to see this. One of the players just blew himself up in Philadelphia."

They all pushed into the crowd to see what was going on. Kevin squeezed his hands around Lindsey's shoulders as they watched. Every breath Lindsey took was harder than the last. The room began to spin. Lindsey could hear the news reporter speak, but the words did not seem real.

"For those of you who are just joining our broadcast, I'm live in Philadelphia, where the New York Mets were scheduled to play the Philadelphia Phillies tonight. That game, however, will be postponed. It seems that one of the Mets players, Julio Sosa, blew himself up leaving one other dead and two others injured. We have identified Aaron Diaz as the second fatality besides Julio Sosa himself. We have not gotten word yet on the two players injured in tonight's tragedy, but as soon as we do, we will get those names to you. It is not clear yet weither the bombing was meant as suicide or if there was criminal intent involved. We have been told that the two deceased were good friends. It is..."

The reporter's words began slurring together until all Lindsey could hear was a dull roar in the background. The room began to spin, and Lindsey felt like she was in a free fall. She couldn't reach out to latch onto anything, because she could not remember how to make her limbs obey. She couldn't react in any way. All she could do was remain frozen in her free fall.

"Lindsey," a voice called. "Lindsey, can you hear me?"

Lindsey could hear the voice but could not respond. Lindsey did not know where the voice was coming from. It was a voice she recognized, but she could not identify it.

"Lindsey. Lindsey. Kevin, get her out of here," the voice said.

When Lindsey came to, she was sitting on the sidewalk outside. Kevin, the Braves short stop, and one of the pitchers were all three standing over her.

"Lindsey, are you ok?" the pitcher asked.

"It isn't real. It can't be. Aaron is ok," Lindsey mumbled.

The short stop sat down beside Lindsey and took her hand in his. "Lindsey, there has been an accident," he said. His eyes were kind but veiled in concern. He was trying to break it to Lindsey slowly, carefully, but that couldn't be right. This couldn't be real. Aaron was not gone. There had not been an accident.

Lindsey jerked her hand back. "No there hasn't. Aaron is ok. You'll see. He'll be down here tomorrow. Just wait. You'll see. He's ok," she insisted.

"Maybe someone should take her home," the pitcher suggested.

"You've both got families to get back to. I'll run her home and make sure she is ok," Kevin said. Then he led Lindsey to his truck.

There was a deadly silence in the truck. That silence carried the whole way to Lindsey's apartment. Kevin did not know what to say or if there was anything to say.

Lindsey stared straight ahead as the entire nightmare replayed over and over in her mind. She heard the broadcaster's words again and again.

Kevin pulled into the parking lot at Lindsey's apartment building. He got out and walked around to help Lindsey out of the truck as the tears started to fall against her will. One tear after another rolled down Lindsey's cheeks. She still felt numb inside. None of it felt real to her yet. She did not understand why she was crying so, but she could not stop herself.

Kevin guided Lindsey up to her apartment. "Lindsey, do you have the key?" he whispered.

Lindsey never felt herself move, but she must have given Kevin the key because he walked with her inside the apartment. Kevin shut the door behind them. Then he took Lindsey to the couch and sat down next to her. There is no telling how long they sat there in silence.

Kevin knew he could not leave Lindsey alone like this, but he did not know what to do for her. Lindsey sat frozen on the couch. She did not understand what was going on.

The tears continued slowly down her face. He hated seeing her upset, and her tears were killing him. She was still staring off into space as if not really there with him. She hadn't come back to reality yet; maybe she was avoiding it. Kevin didn't blame her; he wouldn't want anything tying him to reality if he could help it in a situation like this one. He just wished there was something he could do. He wanted to help her so badly, needed to help her.

Lindsey could not see anything but blurs of light and dark. She could still hear the news report repeating inside her head. Suddenly Lindsey heard what the reporter was saying. For the first time it made sense, and Lindsey began to understand.

"No!" she screamed and started crying hysterically. Lindsey jumped as she felt a hand on her back. She turned and saw Kevin. "Am I dreaming?" she asked hopefully.

Kevin shook his head.

"Oh, no," Lindsey cried. She doubled over in her lap crying. "No, no, no, no," she mumbled. She jumped to her feet. "You said he was safe," Lindsey accused.

Kevin looked stunned. "I... I thought he was."

"But he wasn't, was he?" Lindsey pushed.

"I'm sorry. I don't know what happened," Kevin said ashamedly.

"You let Julio kill him. That's what happened," Lindsey shouted.

"I didn't let Julio do anything. It's hard to stop things I never see coming. I don't understand what happened. What was I supposed to do, Lindsey?" Kevin snapped back losing his temper. They were both yelling now.

"How would I know what to do? It's your job," Lindsey started hitting Kevin in the chest repeatedly and crying hysterically. "It was your job. It was your job. It was your job," she chanted.

Kevin eased Lindsey back down to the couch and sat down beside her. "He's gone, Kevin. He's gone," Lindsey cried softly.

"I'm so sorry, Lindsey. I'm so sorry," Kevin whispered.

"I can't believe he's gone," Lindsey cried breathlessly.

"I know. Shhh," Kevin sighed. He wrapped his arms around Lindsey and held her. Lindsey cried herself to sleep in Kevin's arms. After she fell asleep, Kevin found a blanket to cover her up.

The next morning when Lindsey woke up Kevin was on the phone. "No, sir, none whatsoever... Yes, sir... I know, sir, but I got stuck... No, sir. There is no problem... Yes, sir... Yes, sir. I remember... That's not necessary, sir... Yes, sir, but... No, sir... Yes, sir... Yes, sir," he said.

The one sided conversation made no sense whatsoever, and Lindsey was too drowsy to analyze it or even remember why she should bother.

"What was that about?" she asked.

"Nothing. Go back to sleep. I've got to go to the house right now, but I'll be back later to check on you," Kevin said.

"Do you have to go?"

"Lindsey, I'm in enough trouble as it is. I've got to go home," Kevin replied.

"Please, Kevin. I don't want to be alone," Lindsey pleaded as the events of last night came flooding back to her.

Kevin took a deep breath and let it out. "You can come with me, but we've got to go now," Kevin offered.

Lindsey did not say a word but jumped up and followed him.

Kevin lived at least fifteen minutes across town. The ride started out with the same awkward silence from the night before. Kevin shook his head. "If I make it through this without losing my job, it will be a miracle," he mumbled.

"Because of me?" Lindsey timidly asked.

"No. Of course not," Kevin replied, but Lindsey did not believe him.

"Kevin, I'm sorry I yelled at you last night. I didn't mean any of that. It wasn't your fault," Lindsey apologized.

"I know. Grief can make you say a lot of things you don't mean. Don't worry about it. It has already been forgotten."

It did not take long to get to Kevin's house. When Kevin and Lindsey walked in the house, there was a man already there. He was the same man Lindsey had seen at the hotel the night everything with Nate Fields happened, and Lindsey automatically shied away from him. The man looked annoyed. When he saw Lindsey, however, his expression turned stern and unforgiving.

"What is she doing here?" he asked.

"She was upset," Kevin answered.

"That is not our problem. I asked what she is doing here."

"I couldn't leave her alone."

The man looked at Kevin very seriously without saying a word.

"She knew Aaron Diaz," Kevin said.

"So did many others. I want to know why she is here now with you," the man said.

"She knows who I am," Kevin replied.

"Before Nate Fields? How long?" the man asked.

"Since day one," Kevin answered.

"Why am I only now hearing this?"

"I don't know," Kevin answered.

"You realize that this will have severe consequences. I'm out of tricks, Kevin," the man said.

"Yes, sir," Kevin responded.

"I'm still waiting. What is she doing here?" the man repeated.

"I told you I don't know. I just couldn't leave her. She needed me, so I..." Kevin trailed off.

"You knew better. You brought her here anyway. Do you remember what I asked you that night at the hotel?" the man asked. Kevin nodded. "What was your response?"

"I know what I said," Kevin shot back.

"This is the last time I'll ask. Do we have a problem?" the man asked.

Kevin took a deep breath. "I think so. Yes," he answered with a defeated kind of honesty.

"Do you have a solution to this problem?"

"Does it look like it?" Kevin responded.

"You have until this time tomorrow. Kevin, I'm sorry. I want to know what she knows about this investigation. I want to see everything you have on Julio Sosa and Aaron Diaz. I want to know why we did not see this coming. I want to know how soon we can get baseball back on its regular schedule safely."

Kevin gathered stacks and stacks of papers. The man went through the papers while Kevin explained about Lindsey. He started in the very beginning, where Lindsey was writing FBI reports in Forest Hills. Kevin told the man how Lindsey had recognized him but kept quiet. He reminded the man about the night with Nate Fields and told him that he had not been returning a glove at all. He had been keeping an eye on Lindsey to be sure that she did keep quiet about who he really was. He saw right away that Nate Fields was going to be trouble. Kevin admitted to the man that the only reason he became involved in the Nate Fields incident was to defend Lindsey. Kevin said that Lindsey knew he was not returning a glove but did not say anything. He explained about everything Lindsey had seen set up in his living room and how much of the investigation she knew about.

The man never said a word to interrupt. He only listened and went through papers. When Kevin finished the man looked up at him and asked, "Did you say that this young lady dated Aaron Diaz for some time?"

"Yeah," Kevin answered.

"What did you say her name was?"

"Lindsey Sanders."

"Lindsey, how often did you and Aaron Diaz talk?" the man asked, but Lindsey did not respond. In fact, she did not even realize that the man was addressing her at all. She was lost deep in thought. The truth was that this whole experience still seemed unreal to her. Lindsey was trying to put together in her head the events of last night and its implications in the real world.

"Lindsey," Kevin called, but Lindsey did not respond. "Yo, Sanders," Kevin yelled.

Lindsey jumped as she was snatched from her thoughts.

"Lindsey, did you talk often with Aaron Diaz?" the man asked.

"Yes, sir."

"Did he ever mention Julio Sosa?"

"Yes, sir, Julio was his best friend," Lindsey said. The man looked at Kevin.

"What about Julio's new friends? What did Aaron think about them?" Kevin asked.

"He didn't like them," Lindsey replied.

"Why not?" the man asked.

"He said they were trouble," Lindsey remembered.

"Did Mr. Diaz ever say what kind of trouble?" the man asked.

"He didn't know," Lindsey responded.

"Why did he think they were trouble then?"

"Aaron just had a bad feeling about them. He said Julio was not the same anymore. Julio did not want to spend time with Aaron anymore. Aaron said that when he refused to join Julio and his new friends that Julio called him the enemy," Lindsey told the man.

"The enemy. Mr. Diaz never hinted that he might know what Julio Sosa's new friends were up to?"

"Never."

The man looked back to Kevin. "I can't find anything here that would point to Diaz as a possible target. This sounds more like a personal attack to me," he said.

"That's what I thought, but why at the ball field? Aaron would have met with him anytime, anywhere," Kevin said.

"Maybe he picked a more public area in an attempt to take out more than just his target," the man suggested.

"I doubt it. The stadium isn't open to the public that early, and there would only have been a handful of players on the field that soon," Kevin explained.

Tears started streaming down Lindsey's face. "Maybe he wanted to make an example of Aaron. He could have been warning others who were asking too many questions, pushing too hard against them, or whatever it was that Aaron did wrong," she said.

"She could be onto something," Kevin softly agreed.

"Could be, but how many others are we talking? Who is he trying to warn? If that theory pans out, I need to know who, how many, and where these others are. What we need is someone who can get deep inside without getting caught. If there are others, we can pull information together from them and send in one of our men...

Lindsey, do you know any mutual friends that Diaz and Sosa might have had?" the man asked.

"No, she doesn't," Kevin interrupted the same time Lindsey answered, "Yes, sir."

"No, you don't," Kevin told her firmly.

"Yes, I do," Lindsey insisted.

"You don't know any of them well enough to link them with Julio's new friends. Just stay out of it," Kevin said.

"You do know their mutual friends though? Could you get to know them better and maybe find out what they know about Julio's new friends?" the man requested.

"I'm sure I could," Lindsey replied.

"No, you couldn't. It's dangerous. You don't know what you're doing," Kevin said.

"How hard do you think it would be to get close to them?" the man asked completely ignoring Kevin.

"I've met all Aaron's friends. I don't guess it would be too hard," Lindsey answered.

"This is a great idea. Who would suspect her? She is going through denial and asking a bunch of questions about the deceased," the man explained to Kevin.

"You're using her. This is dangerous. She has no idea what she's getting herself into, and I don't like it," Kevin said.

"I don't remember asking your opinion on the matter," the man said.

"Ben, you arrogant, control freak. It's a lousy idea and you know it," Kevin shouted.

"You better watch who you're talking to like that. As your superior I could have you terminated," the man warned.

"And as my brother?" Kevin asked. The man did not answer. Instead he turned back to Lindsey.

"Would you be willing to help if you were asked to? We would make absolutely sure you are safe. What do you say?" he asked gently. It was the first show of feeling that Lindsey had seen from the man.

This was Lindsey's chance. She could help find the people who killed Aaron. She looked over at Kevin. He was watching her and shaking his head. He did not want Lindsey's help, but that was too bad. She was going to help whether he liked it or not. She was going to help for Aaron's sake. It had nothing to do with Kevin. "I'll do whatever I can to help," Lindsey agreed.

"Ah, thank you. You see, Kevin? There is nothing to discuss," the man said.

"You pompous wind bag, she hardly knows where she is right now. When the reality hits her, she is going to be in a very intense situation that she can't handle. Then what?" Kevin shouted.

"That temper of yours will get you into serious trouble one day," the man said.

"Yeah, yeah. Right after my temper pops that big head of yours," Kevin shot back. The man did not respond. He started toward the door and left.

When the man shut the door behind him Kevin grabbed a phone off a table. He ripped the cord out of the wall and threw the phone at the door. Then he spun around towards Lindsey.

"I know you saw me shaking my head. Did you think I was shaking it for my health? What is your problem? You have no idea what you're getting yourself into. Why couldn't you just listen to me?"

"Why can't I help?" Lindsey asked.

"Because it's dangerous. You have no business doing this kind of stuff, Lindsey. You don't know what you're doing. Look at you. You're already scared, and you're not directly involved in it yet. So far you've only been touched indirectly. What do you think is going to happen when you put yourself right in the middle of everything? You should have listened to me. I was only trying to look out for you," Kevin said.

"I want to do it for Aaron."

"What good will this do Aaron?"

"I can help find the people who killed him," Lindsey replied.

"Lindsey, the one who killed him died with him. What good will this do?"

"Well, maybe I can help. Maybe no one else will have to die."

"Or maybe you'll get yourself killed," Kevin mumbled.

"I heard that, and that man said I would be safe," Lindsey said.

"And you believed him? Ben is a lying, self centered, back stabber. He'll tell you whatever you need to hear to get you to do what he wants. That's his job. He can't guarantee that you'll be safe. These are real bad guys. This isn't make believe, Lindsey. They are evil men, and they are extremely dangerous," Kevin shouted.

"Quit yelling at me. I just want to help," Lindsey shouted back.

Kevin shut his eyes and took a deep breath. Then he opened his eyes and calmly said, "Fine. I'm out numbered, and you're both stubborn and stupid. Go ahead with your insane plans to help, but don't say that I didn't warn you."

Chapter TEN

The series between the Phillies and the Braves was postponed until later in the season. The rest of baseball resumed their regular schedule after only one day of mourning. They wanted to prove that they wouldn't let men like Julio stop them from living life to its fullest, but life would never be quite the same again. Lindsey stuck as close to Kevin as she could. She basically became his second shadow. He was her crutch. She leaned on him for strength.

At night when she went home alone, she cried herself to sleep. She had trouble believing that Aaron was gone. It made her sick to her stomach to think about how he died. Such a gruesome death, it wasn't fair that it should have happened to such a kind person.

The first chance Kevin got he went to visit the two men who were injured in the bombing. Lindsey, being his second shadow, went with him. "Hey, guys. How are y'all doing?" Kevin asked.

"I've been better," one of the players answered. Lindsey looked at both of them lying in hospital beds. They each had severe burns. Their skin was red and puckered in spots and covered with gauze bandages in others. The doctors were not sure yet when they would come off the disabled list. First, they had to focus on getting out of the hospital. She imagined it would be a long, hard road back.

Lindsey watched while Kevin talked with the two players. She could not hear them anymore. She could only stand there and stare. Then everything began to blur as tears welled up in her eyes. She fought the tears back as long as she possibly could. The tears began to stream down her face. "Did you see what happened?" she asked.

"Yes," one of them answered.

"Did he suffer long?" Lindsey asked.

"No. It killed him instantly I think," the player said.

Now there was no holding anything back. The tears poured down Lindsey's face.

"It must have hurt so bad. What happened?" Lindsey asked.

"We were the only three guys from our team there. It was still too early for most of the guys. There were only a handful of Mets players there. Julio Sosa came walking toward our dugout. I didn't think anything of it at the time. Aaron and Julio were good friends. We were headed into the dugout. Aaron turned back to go see what Julio wanted. He met Julio a few feet or so from the dugout. Julio said, 'Lo siento' and hugged Aaron. That's when the bomb exploded. Julio must have had the bomb on him. There was a loud explosion, and it burnt everything around it. When we heard the explosion, we hit the dirt. The doctors say that being that low in the dugout was the only thing that saved us. When we got up, we couldn't see Julio or Aaron anymore, only blood and pieces. There was a lot of screaming. It wasn't long after that the paramedics came and brought us here," the player recited.

He had probably repeated that horrific chain of events for dozens of police and FBI men and women, each time having to relive that gory nightmare. His eyes were filled with tears as he spoke, and he stared straight ahead.

The other player had not said a word till this point. He laid perfectly still in the hospital bed. He closed his eyes as the first player retold the tragedy to Lindsey.

Lindsey was still crying. Her eyes were blood shot and stinging. "What does 'Lo siento' mean?" she asked.

The first player lay in his bed silently. He was American born and knew very little Spanish.

The second player opened his eyes and spoke for the first time. "It means I'm sorry," he said.

"I'm sorry? For what?" Lindsey asked. The room got deathly quiet and all eyes were on Lindsey. "How can you be sorry for killing someone you haven't killed yet? If he was sorry about what he was about to do, then why did he do it? I don't understand. Aaron was a good man, and he would have done anything for Julio. Why be sorry and then kill him?"

Both men lay in the hospital beds now with tears rolling down their cheeks.

"I just wanted to check on the two of you, but I can see we're only making things worse. We better go. Get well soon, guys. Lindsey, let's go," Kevin said softly. Then he gently guided Lindsey out of the hospital.

Lindsey made a list of mutual friends that Aaron and Julio had, that she had met. The list was long, and there were many more that Lindsey had never met. She could write a list twice as long of people Aaron and Julio had talked about who did not even live in the United States.

Kevin took the list of non-U.S. citizens and emailed it to someone to look into while he started locating the others. Most were men and most played ball. Julio had never played for the Braves, and Aaron only played with the Braves for a short time. Therefore, none of the mutual friends were in the immediate area. The majority were from Philadelphia since Julio had played there for some time also. There were a few more in the New York area, and a handful were scattered between other ball clubs.

Lindsey knew almost every move Kevin made regarding the investigation because she stayed by his side so often. She tried not to point out how much she knew, because she did not want Kevin running her off.

Kevin did not say too much about her tagging along behind him. He just let her follow along. She had volunteered to help. She might as well get an idea what she's gotten herself into. Kevin decided to focus first on the mutual friends who did play ball. It would be easier to get to them.

Every time the Braves played the Phillies or the Mets Lindsey always made it a point to talk with Aaron and Julio's friends. They would mostly talk about Aaron. Most of them avoided Julio being brought up. The ones who dared to mutter Julio's name did not stay on the subject long. Lindsey wasn't getting very far, and it was quickly becoming discouraging.

"What am I doing wrong?" Lindsey asked Kevin.

"What do you mean?" he responded.

"I know I'm not any help. I keep talking to these guys, but I haven't found out anything," Lindsey said.

"You're not doing anything wrong. You're not close enough to these guys to find out the kind of information you're expecting to find. People don't exactly air dirty laundry to casual acquaintances," Kevin explained.

"How do you do it?" Lindsey asked.

"I don't get in a hurry. It takes time to earn peoples trust. Just forget about it. It was a stupid idea from the get go," Kevin replied.

"I really want to help though," Lindsey insisted.

"I know you do, and it was a nice thought. It just isn't very feasible," Kevin told her.

"I told that man that I would help," Lindsey said.

"Don't worry about Ben. He's all talk, little action," Kevin responded, but Lindsey had no intentions of giving up. She was doing this for Aaron. It was going to take time. Lindsey could handle that, but she had to get closer to these guys.

Lindsey tried to kick it up a notch or two. It was easier to get close to the single ones, so Lindsey focused in on them first. They had more time to talk to her. She made sure they knew she was going out of her way to spend time with them, and she started flirting every chance she got. Tom Hammins was the first one to respond. He asked Lindsey out to dinner after a day game, and she gladly accepted. Tom pitched with the Phillies. He had been with the Phillies a long time, so he knew both Aaron and Julio well. Aaron had caught for Tom almost two seasons when he died. Tom had worked close with Julio also. Julio was a pitcher, and when he pitched for the Phillies, he and Tom did a lot together.

Lindsey and Tom started out the night talking about baseball. It was a pretty good place to start since they did have that much in common, but the conversation quickly revolved around Tom. Tom was a good pitcher. He did not have a lot of velocity, but he had good location. He had excellent command of the ball. The only thing wrong with his pitching is the big ego that came with it.

Tom talked about himself nearly the whole night long. Lindsey tried to steer the conversation in other directions, but Tom always found a way back to himself. Lindsey tried bringing up Aaron. Tom only wanted to talk about how Aaron caught his terrific pitches.

Lindsey also brought up Julio. Tom compared his pitching to Julio's and talked about how much he taught Julio. Tom apparently did not know much about things he was not directly involved in. This obviously was not going to work. If Tom knew anything about what happened, he was not going to talk about it. He was a lousy date too.

The next guy Lindsey focused in on was Derrick Smith. Aaron had always spoken very highly of Derrick. Derrick played third base and was well known for his power hitting. Lindsey really got his attention when she started flirting. It did not take long at all before he asked her out. Derrick took Lindsey to an unbelievably crowded club. It was very loud and busy. They really could not talk to one another at all.

When Lindsey did get a chance to talk to him, Derrick turned out to be girl crazy and sex driven. All he wanted to talk about was sex, sex, sex. Needless to say, Lindsey got out as quick as she could. Even if Derrick would open up later, Lindsey was not sticking around to find out. Being with Derrick made her uncomfortable.

The next guy Lindsey went out with was the same way, but this one was more aggressive. Macon Moore played left field for the Mets. He was friendly and real outgoing. He had a reputation for being a ladies' man. When Lindsey started showing him the slightest bit of attention, he jumped at the opportunity to take her out. They went out on a mutual off day just before a series between the Braves and the Mets in New York.

The evening started out calmer than the one with Derrick. Macon took Lindsey to a cozy little restaurant. It was down a back road that was secluded and quiet. Macon was very polite, and conversation was interesting. They talked about a little bit of everything including Aaron and Julio.

Macon did not know much about Julio's friends. He knew basically the same things that Aaron had. Julio's friends were real private and did not like him, so he kept his distance. Macon was really open about both Julio and Aaron, but everything he had to say was the same dead end Lindsey had been down a million times before.

After diner Macon took Lindsey to a movie. As soon as the lights went out in the theater, Macon slid his hand around Lindsey's shoulders. There was nothing wrong with that. It was kind of nice. Macon leaned over and kissed Lindsey. Wow. Macon did not believe in wasting time. Macon seemed like a good guy. Lindsey was having fun so far. Kissing wasn't a bad thing until Macon started getting a lot more intense. Ok. Now Lindsey was beginning to feel uncomfortable with Macon too. This is still a first date after all. This is going a little far. What was it with these guys?

Lindsey pushed Macon back. "Not now," she whispered.

Macon backed off immediately. He did seem to be moving things a little fast, but he backed down so quickly when he saw he had gone too far. Lindsey really liked that about Macon, so she let it go for now.

When the movie ended, they headed to a bar with a live band. Bars were not Lindsey's favorite places to go for personal reasons, but still they were having a good time. They were talking and laughing. Macon wasn't a heavy drinker or at least he wasn't tonight.

Macon asked Lindsey to dance. He was a wonderful dancer. They danced for a long time. It wasn't like dancing with Aaron, who just wanted to have fun with it, but Lindsey was really enjoying herself. When they sat back down Macon sat down real close. It made sense at the time. It was hard to hear over the band. Macon leaned over and kissed Lindsey. Oh, here we go again, Lindsey thought.

Macon took things nice and slow, just innocent little kisses. It was actually kind of sweet. Lindsey went along. Before long Macon started getting more intense again. It was not that it did not feel good, he was a good kisser; it just was not appropriate. They had not known each other that long really. No one had kissed Lindsey like that since she and Aaron broke up. For just a minute Lindsey forgot who she was kissing and really liked it.

It only took a minute before Lindsey realized where she was and what was going on. Lindsey pushed him back.

"Macon, slow down," she said.

"Shhh," Macon said and kept going.

Lindsey pushed him back again. "Macon, slow down. This is moving too fast for me," she said.

"You know you like it," Macon said and kept going.

Lindsey pushed him back for a third time. "That's not the point, Macon. Slow down. I'm not ready to move that fast," she said.

Macon ignored her and kept going. Lindsey pushed him off again.

"Macon, stop," she said.

Macon kept going, and this time he started to rub her thigh.

For a fifth time Lindsey pushed him off, but this time she did not have to say a word. Kevin walked up.

"Hi, Lindsey, aren't you going to introduce me?" he asked. Macon turned around to face Kevin. "Oh, hey. Macon, right?" Kevin said.

"Yeah, who are you?" Macon asked, but of course, he already knew who Kevin was. Everyone in baseball knew who Kevin was even if they had not met him yet.

Kevin introduced himself, then pulled up a chair and started talking. Kevin stayed and talked for another couple of hours. Macon kept hinting for Kevin to leave, but Kevin simply ignored Macon the same way Macon had ignored Lindsey.

"I guess I better call it a night if I want to get in some early batting practice tomorrow. Lindsey, do you want to just ride back with me since I'm going to the hotel anyway. It will save Macon a trip," Kevin suggested.

"Sure, if you don't mind," Lindsey answered. Macon looked annoyed, but Lindsey did not care.

Kevin was silent for most of the ride. Lindsey knew from the look on his face that he was not happy with her at all. It was all he could do to hold his tongue.

Lindsey took it for as long as she could. "Say something," she said.

"You have awful taste in men," Kevin said.

Lindsey waited a minute. "Is that all?" she asked.

"What do you want me to say?"

"I don't know. Yell, scream, something, anything. You're mad," Lindsey said, pointing out the obvious.

"I'm not mad," Kevin responded.

"Yes, you are. I can see it in your face. You are mad and the wheels in your head just keep turning. What are you thinking about?"

"I'm not mad, Lindsey. Maybe a little frustrated, but I'm not mad. Honestly, I'm thinking about chaining you to my belt loop. That way when you get yourself into these messes, I can just yank you back. Macon Moore? Lindsey, what were you thinking? That boy has a rep for mess like that. What were you expecting?" Kevin asked.

Lindsey did not know how to answer that without making things worse, so she just kept quiet. The next time, though, Lindsey was going to make sure she knew a little more about the guy first.

Chapter Eleven

Rodney Ramirez was a center fielder with the Phillies. He grew up in Puerto Rico but in a different area from Aaron and Julio. Lindsey had met him a few times with Aaron. He appeared to be well mannered, so Lindsey decided he might be a safer attempt.

It was harder to get Rodney's attention. He was divorced. His first wife had really taken him for a ride, so Rodney was hesitant where women were concerned. Lindsey would talk and flirt with Rodney every time the Braves saw the Phillies. Rodney was always polite, but he never seemed interested.

The last night the Braves and Phillies played one another Rodney finally asked if he could give Lindsey a call sometime during the off season. She had just about given up hope of ever really catching his attention.

The Braves won a division title like tradition, but this time they went on to win the national league championship. The World Series came down to the Braves and the Yankees. In the final game the Braves kept a one run lead straight through till the ninth but could not hold them. They wound up loosing by a final of four to three.

Nevertheless, it had been exciting, and it gave Lindsey and Mr. Parks something to talk about for hours on end.

Rodney did call during the off season. As a matter of fact, he called quite often. They would talk about this and that. Lindsey and Rodney actually found that they had a lot in common. They both liked action movies and a wide variety of music. They both loved karaoke but would not sing in public themselves. They both enjoyed bowling even though Lindsey admitted she was not any good.

Rodney was a bit of a cut up. He loved to make people laugh. They talked all through the off season, but Rodney never once asked her out. They were close enough now that Lindsey could easily get whatever information she wanted, but for the first time since she and Aaron had broken up, she had found someone who she wanted to date.

Spring training got off the ground again, and the Braves looked strong. The first time the Phillies and Braves met up in spring training Lindsey spotted Rodney fast. He was standing in a huddle talking with a mixture of Braves and Phillies players.

"Hey, Lindsey. How's it going," Rodney called.

Lindsey casually joined in the huddle. A little later Kevin and the Braves second baseman joined also. Lindsey hung around as the group slowly dwindled down. Soon Lindsey, Rodney, and Kevin were the only three left. When Kevin finally left, Rodney watched him until he was out of ear shot.

"So how long have you two been dating?" Rodney asked.

"Who?" Lindsey responded.

"You and Kevin."

This took Lindsey by surprise. "Kevin? We aren't dating. We never were," she supplied.

"Really? You spend so much time together. I guess, I just... Are you sure?"

"Yeah, pretty sure. I think I would have noticed something like that," Lindsey answered with a forced laugh.

"Do you think it would be ok it we went out sometime?" he asked.

"Sure," Lindsey responded.

"How about tomorrow night?" Rodney asked.

"That sounds good," Lindsey said.

It's about time! Wow, it's hard to get that man's attention. He took Lindsey out to a nice quiet restaurant. He was very nervous all night long. At the end of the night, Rodney walked Lindsey up to her hotel room and told her good night.

"I had a nice time," Lindsey told him, and she had. Rodney was a perfect gentleman. He opened all doors for Lindsey including car doors. He was as sweet and polite as he could ever have been. Lindsey sincerely enjoyed his company. He was not his usual cut up self, but they talked and talked. She had not had that much fun since she and Aaron first broke up.

Rodney was uncharacteristically jumpy. He kissed Lindsey's cheek and left. Well, that was one way to end the evening.

Lindsey stepped inside and flipped on the light. She screamed when she saw someone sitting in her room. "Kevin! You scared me half to death. What are you doing? How did you get in here?" she asked.

"You think you're real clever. Don't you?" he said.

"What are you talking about?"

"First Tom, then Derrick and Macon, and now Rodney," Kevin said.

"What? I'm not allowed to date now?"

"Don't try to play little miss innocent with me. I may not know them very well, but I don't think they are your type."

"Is that so, and what is my type?" Lindsey asked.

"How should I know, but I'm sure the first three were a little wild even for you," Kevin replied.

"What about Rodney?"

"You're not going to turn this around on me. They all just happened to play for either the Phillies or the Mets just like Julio and Aaron? You're not fooling anyone," Kevin said.

"I don't know what you're talking about. For your information, it just so happens that I had a fantastic time tonight. Thank you very much," she told him.

"Well, please, tell me all about it then," Kevin said sarcastically.

Lindsey knew that he was only trying to be cute, but she was going to make him regret saying it. She went and sat down next to him.

"It was so wonderful. Rodney is such a sweet guy. He opened the car door for me. He took me to a real nice restaurant. It had a quiet, elegant atmosphere. He even pulled out the chair for me to sit down. He was so gentleman like.

"He was nervous too. We talked a lot during the off season, and he was still so nervous. It was actually kind of flattering. We talked all night long. The conversation did not revolve around him. I hated that about Tom. We were both interested in the topics. I loved that. We have so much in common. It just makes him so easy to talk with. Plus, he wasn't trying to get in my pants all night like Derrick or Macon. Rodney is the total opposite from them. As a matter of fact, he kissed my cheek when he kissed me good night."

"Oh, he kissed your cheek. He's really bringing out the big guns now," Kevin teased.

"Stop it, Kevin. It was sweet in its own way. He was nervous, and he's trying to take things slow," Lindsey defended.

"Oh, yeah. He's taking it slow alright. He's almost not moving at all," Kevin laughed.

"Shut up! He's getting over his wife," Lindsey explained.

"I guess you could do worse than Rodney Ramirez," Kevin gave in with a resigned sigh. "Rodney's a good guy, but next time don't go vigilante on me. If you're determined to go through with this, talk to me at least. If you keep jumping from one player to the next until you've dated both teams, someone is going to get suspicious."

"I'm not going to date both teams," Lindsey replied. Rodney was the last one that Lindsey knew of, who was single anyway.

The second date went a little smother. Rodney was not as nervous. He was still a gentleman and very sweet. At the end of the date, he gave her a real kiss, not a peck on the cheek. He gave her a real life mouth to mouth, breath taking kiss. It turns out that Rodney was a great kisser to boot. His ex-wife was an idiot to give him up. By the end of March, Rodney and Lindsey were talking on the phone everyday that they could not see each other. They got real close real fast.

The first series of the regular season that the Braves played the Phillies was in Philadelphia. Their first day together, Lindsey and Rodney drove past Aaron's house. "Rodney, do you ever think about Aaron?" Lindsey asked.

"Yeah, sometimes. How can you not? It was so absurd. I wish I knew what was going through Julio's mind. What kind of thoughts has a man got to have to kill himself and his best friend too? I can't imagine," Rodney said.

"Me either. Sometimes it's still hard to believe. Aaron was my friend. It hurts to think of him being gone. I didn't know Julio that well. What was he like?" Lindsey asked.

"Julio? Oh, he was great. He was a lot like Aaron actually. Those two were like brothers. They were inseparable. At least they were until right before," Rodney said.

"What happened?" Lindsey asked.

"I don't know. Julio stopped wanting to cut up and have a good time. He used to be such a comedian. He started getting serious all the time. He never cracked a smile anymore. Then he quit hanging out with us. I didn't really talk to him much after that. Aaron still talked with him for a little while longer. Then after a while, he quit talking to Aaron too, but I don't know why. I never asked him what was up. I wish I had. I just never dreamed Julio could do something so terrible. I can't help wondering sometimes if I could have stopped him. If I had asked him what was bothering him, maybe I could have helped in some way. I was an awful friend," he explained.

"Don't say that. You're not an awful friend. You couldn't have known," Lindsey said.

"No, I am. Mike. You know Mike. Mike Rodregiaz. He was one of the guys who got burnt from the explosion. He told me that Julio said 'lo siento' just before the bomb went off. That means I'm sorry. I'm sorry, Lindsey. Do you know what that says to me? It says he was hurting. He was looking for help but couldn't find any," Rodney told her.

"Rodney, don't do this to yourself. It wasn't your fault. Besides suicide victims don't usually take others out with them," Lindsey said.

"What are you saying?" Rodney asked.

"This was an absurdly unusual case. You can't play a game of what if's," Lindsey said.

"I guess you're right. Let's talk about something different though," he said.

Lindsey and Rodney never talked about what happened with Aaron and Julio again, but that did not stop Lindsey. She still talked with everyone else she could find who had known Aaron and Julio.

Soon she had asked every member of the Phillies and the Mets the same set of questions "How well did you know Julio? Did you see anything like that coming? Do you understand why he did it? Could you ever imagine doing something like that?"

Lindsey routinely got the same set of answers from everyone. Some knew Julio better than others. No one ever claimed to know any of his friends outside of baseball. Absolutely no one saw it coming or understood why it happened. A few admitted that they had contemplated suicide before themselves, but no one would ever think of taking a friend out of this world with them.

A few of the men questioned made comments about Lindsey asking too many questions. Kevin always followed up on those. Most turned out to be dead ends. On the other hand, a couple did pan out, and Kevin put them under close surveillance.

Mike Rodriguez was the one exception to the usual set of answers. He had been there to witness the gruesome event. He had scars to show for it, both physical and emotional. Mike did not talk much about what happened that day. Every time he did, he got choked up.

"I can't get the picture out of my head. It's like a terrifying nightmare that keeps repeating," he said. Mike swore that he never saw it coming. "If I had I wouldn't have put myself so close. That may sound awful, but I would not have stayed to get hurt," he said.

"You need to stop asking everyone so many questions," Kevin said.

"Why? It's working. I found you two leads. Didn't I?" Lindsey argued.

"Yes, but at what expense?"

"What to you mean?"

"Do you really think those are the only two out there? Not everyone is stupid enough to act defensive when you start asking questions. That just screams I'm doing something wrong. Most of these men are smart. Real smart. Instead of drawing attention to themselves, they are going to watch you. They will want to know where you are and what you are doing at all times. Now you've put yourself in the middle of a firing range and compromised my cover," Kevin said.

"How did I compromise your anything?" Lindsey asked.

"You're asking too many questions. You either believe in letting your enemy know you're coming or you're running back to tell someone. In case you're running to tell, they are going to find out who you talk to on a daily basis, and who do you talk to on a daily basis?" Kevin asked.

"I talk to a lot of the guys everyday. Who am I telling, the entire Braves ball club?" Lindsey asked.

"You don't believe that. Who do you spend the most time with?" Kevin asked.

"You, I guess, but there could be any number of explanations for that," Lindsey defended.

"Like what? I see you more than Rodney does," Kevin challenged.

"Well, at least I'm trying. Don't you have anything better to do than correct me all the time?" Lindsey asked.

"Sure I do, but this takes less time. I ran into Katrina last week," Kevin said with a failed attempt at casualness.

"Katrina who?" Lindsey asked.

"Katrina Ramirez."

"Rodney's ex-wife?"

Kevin nodded.

"What did she want?"

"I don't know. Nothing, I guess. She said she was looking for Rodney," Kevin replied.

"What did she want, more blood?" Lindsey demanded defensively.

"Didn't sound like it to me. She said she wanted to talk to Rodney about coming back home. You know she's not officially his ex-wife. Don't you?" Kevin asked.

"I thought they were divorced," Lindsey said.

"No. Rodney never signed the divorce papers. Apparently, Katrina and her lawyer never pushed it. They are still legally married," Kevin said.

"Are you lying?" Lindsey pushed.

Kevin shook his head.

"They are still married?" Lindsey asked indignantly.

Kevin nodded.

"You really saw Katrina?"

Kevin nodded still not saying a word.

"She really said all that?"

 Again, Kevin nodded.

"This is ridiculous. There has to be a perfectly rational explanation for this," Lindsey said.

"Ok, but don't say I didn't give you fair warning," Kevin told her.

Lindsey decided to wait things out. There had to be a reason Rodney never said anything before. All Lindsey had to do was wait and see what happened. What else could she do?

A couple of days later Rodney did finally mention Katrina. Rodney called really late. "Hey, what's up?" Lindsey asked.

"Not much. I'm doing some thinking. Katrina just left," Rodney replied.

"Your ex-wife?"

"Well not exactly," Rodney admitted.

"What does 'not exactly' mean?" Lindsey questioned.

"We're still married. I guess I never signed the divorce papers. I kept putting it off. It was just too hard. I guess when I started moving on, I sort of forgot about them. Now she wants to get back together, but I don't think so. I just started putting my life back together," Rodney explained.

"Do you love her?" Lindsey asked.

"Of course I love her. That's why I married her in the first place, but how can I just forgive and forget everything she put me through?" Rodney asked.

"I think you already have," Lindsey replied.

The other end of the line went silent.

"Lindsey," was all he said, but his voice said so much more.

"I know. Go call her," Lindsey interrupted.

Lindsey was not sure what to do now. Rodney lied. She should be furious. She must be out of her mind. She had just helped her boyfriend get back together with his ex-wife. No, she helped her very wonderful, almost perfect boyfriend stay with his wife. Lindsey got in her car and started driving. She did not know where to go, but she had to get out of the apartment. She ended up at Kevin's house.

Lindsey did not bother going to the front door and ringing the door bell. Kevin never kept the garage door locked when he was home. Lindsey walked right inside.

The house was dark. She could not hear a sound. She did not call out for Kevin. She didn't make any noise at all just started walking through the house looking for him. She was headed toward the bedroom when Kevin jumped in front of her with a gun pointed right at her.

Lindsey did not jump. She did not scream. She did not react at all. "Oh, Lindsey," Kevin sighed. He pulled the gun back. "What are you doing sneaking around in the middle of the night?"

Lindsey did not move. She did not say a word.

"What's going on? What's wrong?" Kevin asked almost desperately.

"I talked to Rodney," Lindsey said and did not say another word.

She did not try to explain. She did not try to move, and Kevin did not ask her to. He wrapped his arms around her and stayed. He didn't move. He didn't speak. For a long time, they simply stood there in complete silence.

"Come on," Kevin said breaking the silence. He led Lindsey back to his bed and covered her up. Then he sat down beside her until she fell asleep.

Elizabeth Lee Sorrell

Chapter TWELVE

The next morning when Lindsey woke up, she went to find Kevin. She found him in the living room asleep on the couch. Lindsey walked over and quietly laid her hand on his chest. Kevin woke up with a jump. "You're getting good at scaring me, kid. You look better today," he said as he sat up on the couch.

"I don't feel better," Lindsey admitted.

"Want to tell me what happened?" Kevin asked.

"I did it," she said sitting down next to him. Then Lindsey proceeded to give Kevin her whole phone call with Rodney verbatim.

"Wow. He really loves her?" Kevin asked.

Lindsey nodded.

"You did the right thing," Kevin assured her.

"Then why do I feel so lousy?"

"The right thing is not always the easy thing. Sometimes doing the right thing can hurt real bad," Kevin answered.

Kevin convinced Lindsey to chill out with her man hunt. Getting close to these people was not working for her. She got burnt pretty badly trying to get close to Rodney. Plus, she had already talked to everyone there was to talk to anyway. She needed to take a little time off.

Lindsey dove head first into the season at hand. She devoted all her time and thoughts fully to the Braves. They won the division title. They won the National League championship and moved on to the World Series with the Yankees.

The first game was an intense one. The starting pitchers were going head to head. The score was tied nothing, nothing going into the seventh. In the top of the seventh with two outs and two men on base, the Yankees hit a home run to make the score three to nothing, but the Braves came back fighting in the bottom of the seventh. The short stop hit a lead off home run. After a loud fly out, the one home run was all the Braves could come up with. In the ninth inning Kevin hit a solo home run followed by a base hit by the catcher, but back to back strike outs ended the inning. The Braves lost by a final score of three to two.

In the second game the Braves hit fast and hard. The lead off hitter hit a double followed by another hit to move him to third. Another single drove in the first run of the day for the Braves. A home run scored three more runs. The first baseman got a triple and scored on a sacrifice ground out. There was one more hit, but a double play ended the inning. No more runs were scored after that for either team. The Braves held the Yankees for a final of five to zero.

In the end it all came down to game seven. The rubber game would decide the next world champions. The first half of the last game saw a lot of action. The braves showed off their dynamic defense in the top of the second to keep the Yankees from scoring. An infield throwing error for the Yankees put the lead off man on first for the Braves. A hit and walk loaded the bases. Then what the Braves meant to be a sacrifice bunt went bad when the runner was called out at home. With the bases still loaded the catcher hit a ball to straight away center. It looked like it was going out, but the Yankees center fielder leaped up and pulled it back in for an out.

In the top of the third the Yankees got one solo home run. In the bottom a triple, a single, and a home run made the score three to one, Braves. Then in the top of the fifth back to back hits, a walk and a grand slam put the Yankees back on top five to three. Nothing else happened leaving the final score three to five, Yankees. The Yankees left the world champions, again.

Lindsey stayed out real late with Kevin and a couple of other guys after the loss. Lindsey had not packed to go back to Forest Hills yet, but she could do that tomorrow. She was exhausted when she got home at four that next morning, so she went straight to bed.

She only got two hours sleep because the door bell started ringing at six. Who in their right mind would be ringing someone's door bell at six in the morning? Lindsey was surprised when she got to the door and saw Mike Rodriguez. They had never even met until everything happened with Aaron and Julio.

"I'm sorry if I woke you. I was wondering if we could talk. I know it's early. I'm going back to Philadelphia today, and I didn't want to leave without getting a chance to talk with you. Please, it would mean so much to me. It's about what happened with Aaron and Julio," Mike said.

"Sure, come on in," Lindsey welcomed.

"I know that you've been asking around a lot, trying to piece together what went wrong. I was wondering if you had anything figured out," Mike said.

"No. Nothing. Everyone's answers are always the same. No one knew Julio was to that point. It was like he never reached out for help at all. Nobody had any idea how bad he was hurting. The strange part is no one can figure why he was hurting. He was in a high point of his career. He had friends. He had family back home. The part I don't understand is why Aaron. Aaron was a good guy. He thought the world of Julio. What did Aaron do that he deserved to die for?" Lindsey asked.

"I don't know. Julio did not look mad or upset in the least. He looked as normal as he ever did," Mike's eyes started swelling up with tears. "He was cool and calm. He spoke with ease. He said 'lo siento' and hugged Aaron like everything was good. The next thing I knew Julio was exploding. There was blood and fire everywhere. You and Aaron were close. He never said anything?" Mike asked.

"No, not a word. He loved Julio too much. He never would have let Julio kill himself. Aaron would have done whatever he had to do to find Julio the help he needed. If Aaron had seen Julio's suicide coming, he wouldn't have let it happen," Lindsey replied confidently.

"Had they been fighting or anything?"

"Well, not really. Julio had been trying to alienate himself. Aaron was very concerned about him, but they were not fighting."

"Do you think maybe Julio did not mean it as a suicide attempt, but more of an attack against Aaron?"

"No! Of course not. Never. Why would Julio want to do that?" Lindsey reacted.

"I don't know. I've had a lot of time to think about this. It's all I can ever think about. I want to make sense of it so bad. I can't make myself move on without some kind of closure, and I can't find closure for something I just can't understand.

"I've tried the suicide approach, but why would he kill Aaron? I've tried the murder approach, but why would he kill himself at the same time? I've heard of cases where the murderer feels so guilty afterwards that he turns the gun on himself, but Julio and Aaron's death were timed perfectly together. It wasn't one then the next.

"Why premeditate a murder that you felt that guilty about before you even committed it? It just doesn't make sense. I thought at one time Julio could have done it for attention, but what good would the attention do him? He isn't here to see it. I can't make heads or tales of anything. How are you dealing so well?" Mike asked.

"I don't try to take it more than one day at a time for starters. I lost both my parents in a car crash, so dealing with death is nothing new for me. It helps to have someone there in case you need to talk or if you don't feel like talking at all.

"I have Kevin. He's been really great. I couldn't have asked for a better friend. He doesn't try to make it go away or pretend it never happened. He's always been there for me. Other than that, I guess I've just tried to stay busy," Lindsey explained.

"Is that why you've been dating so much?" Mike asked.

"What?"

"It's no secret that you've been getting around the Phillies' ball club. You've dated almost every single or separated man on the team, but nothing seems to last. Is that your way of filling the void?" Mike asked.

Mike's comments took Lindsey by shock. Kevin had been right. Not only was she drawing attention to herself, she was making a reputation for herself as well.

"I never thought about it before. I have been dating a good bit though. Maybe it is. How do you fill the void?" Lindsey asked.

"I don't know yet, but when I find something, I'll let you know. Thank you, Lindsey. I don't feel so alone anymore. I was watching everyone else move on with their lives. It's comforting to know that I'm not the only one having a difficult time," Mike said.

"You're not alone. How about I give you my number? Anytime that you start to feel alone again, I want you to give me a call. We can help each other," Lindsey offered.

Lindsey had no idea how hard Mike was taking it. It had been over a year, and Mike was just now starting to talk about what happened. He had been trying to deal with this all on his own. He was not coping well at all. Mike did not call once during the off season. Lindsey made plans to visit him before the start of spring training. She wanted to check on Mike, because she was so very worried about him.

Mike acted happy to see her and invited Lindsey inside right away. There were empty beer bottles everywhere. Dirty dishes were piled up. Dirty clothes were scattered here and there. Empty pizza boxes, burger wrappers, French fry boxes, all kinds of trash were tossed in the floor, not that much of the floor was visible through all the trash. There was an awful, horrific odor coming from somewhere. The smell permeated the entire house. To call Mike's house nasty would be an understatement. Lindsey was scared to sit down. She knew that not all bachelors were all that good at housekeeping, but this was ridiculous. "I was wondering how you were doing," she said.

"I'm doing much better I found something to fill the void," Mike told her.

"That's great. What did you find?"

Mike picked up a half drunk beer and chugged the rest down. "I found beer," he said holding up the empty bottle.

A pile of clothes started to move next to Lindsey's feet. She screamed and jumped away.

"Oh, I have a dog somewhere. I don't think she likes the mess though. I used to be a neat freak," Mike said.

"What happened?"

"I stopped caring."

A brown dog squirmed its way out from under the clothes. "There she is," Mike exclaimed.

She was the cutest cocker spaniel Lindsey had ever seen. "Oh, she's adorable. What's her name?" Lindsey asked.

"Baby," Mike answered. Lindsey played with the dog a minute.

"Well, I guess I need to get going. I just wanted to check on you," Lindsey said.

Lindsey left more worried than ever. Mike was not dealing with what happened. He was trying to forget what happened. No one should live in that sort of filth. How could a pronounced neat freak live there? Lindsey did not talk to Mike at all during spring training. She tried every time the Braves and Phillies played one another. Mike would always be the last one to the park and the first one to leave. Many of the Phillies players remembered what happened to Aaron and Julio, so Mike's unusual and distant behavior concerned them.

The Braves first trip to Philadelphia this season, Lindsey made a point to visit Mike. When she arrived at Mike's house Rodney was there banging on the door. "I know you're in there, Mike. Talk to me," he screamed.

"What's going on?" Lindsey asked.

"It's Mike. He doesn't talk to anyone anymore. He doesn't ever leave his house except for the games. He's acting strange. I should have done something to stop what happened to Aaron and Julio. I'm not going to stand back and lose another friend like that. I've been here for ten minutes, and he won't answer the door. Stand back," Rodney said.

Rodney kicked the door in. That was a little extreme. What had pushed him to that limit? Lindsey did not know what was going on, but now she was scared. She followed Rodney inside as he ran from room to room calling Mike's name. They ran into the bedroom.

"Mike," Rodney yelled.

"You're trespassing. Get out before I call the cops," Mike hollered from inside the closet. His voice was slurred, making him hard to understand.

"Mike, I'm worried about you. Come out of there. Let me see that you are ok. I want to talk," Rodney begged.

"I said get out," Mike screamed.

"Mike, please," Lindsey said.

"Lindsey, is that you?"

"Yes," she answered.

"What are you doing here?"

"I came to see you."

"Why?"

"I haven't talked with you since spring training. I wanted to check on you," Lindsey replied.

"Did you come with Rodney?" Mike asked.

"No, he was here when I got here. He's worried about you. Mike, you're scaring me," Lindsey said.

"Tell him to go away," Mike ordered.

"I'm not doing that," Rodney said.

"I'm not coming out," Mike responded.

"I'm coming in," Lindsey said.

Rodney grabbed her arm. "No," he whispered.

Lindsey shot him an evil look. "I'm fine," she whispered back.

Lindsey walked in the closet and shut the door back behind her. "Wow. Mike, I can't see you," she said.

"I'm straight back," he replied. Lindsey put her hands out in front of her and slowly crept forward. She ran into Mike's outstretched hand. He took hold of her hand and said, "Push through the clothes."

Lindsey pushed through the clothes that were hanging in front of her and sat down beside Mike. "What are you doing?" she asked.

"I'm hiding in the only clean room left," he answered.

"We can fix that. I can help you clean the house, but why are you hiding?" she asked.

"I couldn't do it. I'm not as strong as you," Mike answered.

"You couldn't do what?"

"I couldn't fill the void and deal with everyday life. I tried dating like you. It didn't help. I tried beer. It didn't help. I dated everyone in sight. I had one one-night stand after another, but I'm more alone than ever. I drank all day long. All I have to show for it is a mess that only drives me crazier each day," Mike explained.

"Mike, I never said I was having one night stands. I never slept with any of them. I've never slept with anyone," Lindsey said.

"You're a virgin?"

"Yes."

"So I did all that for nothing?" Mike asked.

"I guess so. None of that will help. You're only pushing yourself further away from the rest of the world," Lindsey explained.

"I don't know what to do. Will you help me?" Mike asked.

"Sure I will, but first, we have to get out of this closet," Lindsey told him.

They stood up still hand in hand and walked out of the closet together. Mike froze when he saw Rodney. "Rodney, he's fine now. You can go on. I know you want to get to the field. We'll be there in just a little while," Lindsey said.

"Are you sure?" Rodney asked. Lindsey nodded, and Rodney left.

"Look at this place. What have I done?" Mike asked.

"It's ok. It will be just fine. Go get ready. Let's get you to the ball park. Tomorrow is an off day. We will get everything back in order tomorrow. Until then it will just have to stay. Hurry. You don't want to be late," Lindsey urged.

Lindsey came over bright and early the next morning as promised. Mike was already up and trashing beer bottles. "You look better this morning," Lindsey noticed.

"I feel better. Thank you," Mike replied.

"Which way is the washer and dryer? I'll start gathering clothes," Lindsey said. Mike showed Lindsey where the washer and dryer were.

There was a hamper full before Lindsey started gathering clothes from the rest of the house. Lindsey started the first load, and then went to gather clothes. It took forty-five minutes to get all the dirty clothes into the laundry room. They were strewn from one end of the house to the next. It was strange that there were so many clothes everywhere and still so many hanging in the closet yesterday.

By the time Lindsey finished gathering all the dirty clothes, Mike had finished throwing away the empty beer bottles and had started hauling dishes back to the kitchen. The dishes were just as scattered as the clothes had been. Lindsey loaded the dishwasher and started it. Then she helped Mike bring back dishes. "Are you sure you're a neat freak?" Lindsey asked.

"Well, I was at one time. Guess I'll have to get used to the opposite," Mike said grinning.

"Yeah, I guess so. You haven't been so neat lately," Lindsey teased.

"You know what? This is the first time I've smiled since... well, you know," Mike said.

"Feels pretty good. Doesn't it?" Lindsey asked.

"Yeah it does," Mike answered.

They made one quick trip into town to get more dish detergent, laundry detergent, fabric softener, and cleaning supplies. Afterwards they worked hard all day. They went straight on until ten that night. It had been a long day, but it was worth it. The house looked new again. "Oh my goodness. I am exhausted," Lindsey said as they plopped down on the couch.

"I'm too tired to move," Mike agreed.

"You better get some rest. When the Phillies lose to the Braves tomorrow, I don't want to hear any excuses about being warn out from cleaning," Lindsey said.

"Oh, you are hilarious, Lindsey," Mike said sarcastically.

"Who's joking? Y'all are going down," Lindsey taunted.

"Uh-huh. We'll see about that," Mike replied.

"You got that right. I'm going to sit and watch every play while y'all get beat down," Lindsey said.

"You're lucky I'm so tired," Mike said.

"Why is that?"

"Because if I could move, I'd show you how games are won," Mike said.

"Oh-whoa, big talk from someone who can't lift his own arm," Lindsey said.

"Did you ever play?"

"Baseball?"

"No, Lindsey, soccer," Mike said sarcastically.

"Yeah, all the way though school," Lindsey answered.

"What position?"

"Third," Lindsey replied.

"Were you any good?"

"I wasn't terrible."

"What is that supposed to mean? I asked if you were any good. I didn't ask how bad you were. Were you any good?" Mike asked again.

"Yes," Lindsey responded.

"Wow. How big is your head, Lindsey?" Mike teased.

"I cannot win no matter what with you. Yes, I was good. I was real good, but I should have been. Baseball is my life. I ate, slept, and breathed baseball. If I wasn't asleep or in school, I was playing ball year round. I spent more time practicing than anyone I've ever known. I don't mean to be boastful. I worked hard to be that good," Lindsey said.

"Was good? You don't play anymore?" Mike asked.

"No."

"Why not?"

"I don't know. There isn't a team to play on now, and there hasn't really been time since my parents died."

"What happened to your parents?"

"They were in a car accident."

"Well, I know that. Did they get hit? Did they hit something or someone? Were they killed instantly or was it a later result of the crash? There are so many possibilities when you say car crash. What happened?" Mike repeated.

"They were hit by a drunk driver. They were dead when the ambulance got there. The drunk driver was rushed to the hospital, but he died before they could get there. He wasn't even from Forest Hills. No one knew who he was or what he was doing in Forest Hills," Lindsey explained.

"Why haven't you played ball since they died?" Mike asked.

"I didn't go to college. There wasn't a team for me," Lindsey said defensively.

"Maybe you aren't the expert you think you are on dealing with death," Mike accused.

"I never claimed to be an expert," Lindsey snapped.

"If baseball was really your life, why didn't you try to get an adult team started? You do travel with the Braves now. Why don't you ask some of them to throw the ball around with you every once in a while? You still love the game or you wouldn't be here today. Why did you give up on playing?" Mike asked.

"I didn't. I just never gave it as much thought as you. I assumed my chance was over," Lindsey responded.

"Prove it. You and me right now. The city park is ten minutes from here. Get up and let's go play ball," Mike challenged.

"Now? I'm tired. It's almost eleven o'clock. You're crazy," Lindsey whined.

"Chicken. You think I can out hit you," Mike taunted.

"No, I'm sure you can out hit me. Let's go," Lindsey said.

They played, cut up, and had fun till two in the morning. When they got back to the house, they barely drug themselves to the couch.

"Now I'm really too tired to move. Let's do something else," Mike joked.

"No. No more of your crazy ideas. I'm tired, and now I'm sore," Lindsey moaned.

"Aww. Poor thing. Try not to get writer's cramp sitting in the stands tomorrow," Mike teased.

"Shut up," Lindsey said. They both fell fast asleep on the couch and didn't move till morning.

Chapter Thirteen

"Crap! Lindsey, get up. It's noon. We fell asleep," Mike cried.

Lindsey rushed back to the hotel to get ready. Then she hurried to the ball park. Both teams were warming up by the time Lindsey got to the field. She had never been that late. She usually did interviews before the game but not today. It was a close game until the ninth inning when the Braves pulled ahead.

"Where have you been? I haven't seen you since we got in town," Kevin said.

"I went to check on Mike. It was a good thing I did. He was really having a rough time. Yesterday I helped him clean. We cleaned all day long," Lindsey said.

"I went by your room this morning. Where were you?"

"Why am I getting the third degree?"

"Where were you?" Kevin repeated.

"I am a grown woman. This is ridiculous. We were tired from cleaning all day, and we accidentally fell asleep on the couch. Happy dear?" Lindsey snapped.

"Lindsey, I need to know where you are," Kevin said.

"You're not my father," Lindsey interrupted.

"I know that," Kevin started, but Lindsey did not want to hear anything else he had to say. She stormed off before he had time to finish.

Lindsey went for a walk to calm down. She was not paying any attention to where she was going, and she bumped right into Mike. "Yesterday you pulled me back from the edge, and today you can't see me at all. You sure forget people fast," Mike commented.

"I'm sorry, Mike. I'm upset and wasn't looking where I was going," Lindsey apologized.

"I see that. What happened?"

"Oh, nothing. I just got into an argument with Kevin. It was a silly thing to fight over, I guess," Lindsey explained.

"I was going to get something to eat," Mike said.

"Alone?" Lindsey questioned.

"Unless you'd like to join me," Mike replied.

"Sure," Lindsey said.

"Do you always eat alone?" Lindsey asked after they were seated.

"Nah, but who feels like going out after a loss?"

"I told you y'all were going to take a loss today. Didn't I?"

"I think that the game was a little closer than you..." Mike started. A woman slapped Mike hard across the face as she walked past. She never said a word, just kept on walking.

Lindsey was stunned to say the least. "What was that about?" she asked.

"I think we had a one night stand," Mike answered.

"You think? Mike! You can't remember? That's awful," Lindsey scolded.

"There towards the end they got a little foggy. I was drinking too much. Come on. You've never woken up the next morning with regrets?" Mike asked.

"No. I told you I don't sleep around," Lindsey replied.

"Are you serious?"

"Yes," Lindsey answered.

"Never?"

Lindsey shook her head.

"Are you telling me that you have never had sex? Not once?"

"Exactly," Lindsey said.

"How?"

"I just made the decision when I was younger to wait."

"Wow. Better you than me. No! That's not what I meant. I mean... good for you. I could never do it," Mike backtracked.

"Sure you could, if you really wanted to," Lindsey said.

"Well, that leaves me out. Who wants to give up sex? Well, besides you. Um... I'm digging a hole here that I can't get out of. Can we change the subject now?" Mike asked with a chuckle.

"Please," Lindsey responded.

"So, um... nice weather today. Huh?" Mike said.

Lindsey laughed at Mike's useless attempt to change the subject.

"Never?" he asked.

Lindsey could not stop laughing long enough to answer.

"Do you ever... no. Never mind. Wow. Um... did you make it to the park in time today?" Mike asked.

Lindsey nodded while she calmed down her laughter. "Yes. I wasn't in time for interviews, but I was there for the game," Lindsey answered.

After they finished eating Mike gave Lindsey a ride back to the hotel. They did not see one another after the final game. It was get away day for both teams.

Kevin was unusually quiet. He did not act mad or upset in any way. He just was not talking.

"What's the matter?" Lindsey asked.

"Nothing. Why?" Kevin asked.

"You're quiet," Lindsey replied.

"Just because I'm quiet doesn't mean there is something wrong. Couldn't I just be thinking?"

"Ok, you're right. What are you thinking about?"

"No one thing in particular."

"I give up."

"I saw you having dinner with Mike the other night. When did y'all get so close?" Kevin asked.

"I don't know. It was a gradual thing. It's nice to have someone to talk to who's having to deal with everything that happened same as I am. What's wrong with me being friends with Mike?"

"There is nothing wrong with it. I didn't realize the two of you had gotten so close so fast. That's all. I'm glad you're making new friends," Kevin said.

"Yeah, me too. Hey, do you think on the next off day you might want to throw a ball around a little?"

"With you?" Kevin asked surprised.

"You don't have to," Lindsey said.

"No, of course I will. I'd love to. I didn't think you played anymore."

Kevin and Lindsey started playing ball a lot during their off time. A few of the other guys even started joining in. Not all of the coaches were real fond of the idea, but no one tried to stop them.

They took it easy, nothing too intensive. It was a just a chance to blow off a little steam in a nice, healthy sort of way, and Lindsey had the added bonus of playing the game she loved so much.

Lindsey had forgotten how much she loved playing baseball. She had not played in years. Plus, she was playing with a bunch of men who happened to be professional ball players.

Lindsey did not even begin to compare to the others, but she had fun just the same. There was a little friendly competition but nothing too serious.

The next series with the Phillies was played in Atlanta. The Braves had a good record against the Phillies this season. Lindsey got to the park early for the first game. She was hoping to get a few interviews, but Mike tracked her down first.

"Hey, Lindsey. How are you doing?" he greeted.

"Well, hey stranger. I'm doing good. How about you?" Lindsey returned.

"I'm hanging in there. I heard you like karaoke," Mike said.

"Where did you hear that?"

"I've been talking to Rodney. There is a small karaoke place about forty minutes from here. I was wondering if you wanted to check it out tonight after the game. I know Rodney said you usually go out with Kevin after the games. He's more than welcome to come too, if you're interested," Mike offered.

"That sounds awesome. Thank you. I'll ask Kevin as soon as I see him," Lindsey replied.

"Ok then. I better get going. I'll see you after the game," Mike said.

Kevin's timing was impeccable. He walked up just as Mike was leaving. "You're here early. Aren't you?" Kevin asked.

"Yeah. I'm trying to get some extra interviews since y'all are playing so well against the Phillies this year. I just talked to Mike," Lindsey said.

"Oh, good. I know I'll sleep better tonight," Kevin interrupted.

"What crawled up your shorts, cranky?" Lindsey shot.

"Nothing. What were you saying?"

"Mike invited us to go with him tonight to some karaoke place."

"Us?" Kevin inquired.

"Yes. He invited you too, so lose the attitude will you. What's your problem lately anyway?"

"I don't have a problem," Kevin replied.

"Yes, you do. You have been almost unbearable lately," Lindsey told him.

"Can we talk about this later?"

"Yeah, whatever. Are you going tonight?"

"Are you?"

"Yes," Lindsey answered.

"I wouldn't miss it," Kevin said.

They took Kevin's truck that night. Mike and Lindsey talked and laughed well over an hour, and Kevin barely said two words the whole time. He just sat there looking miserable. He might as well have poked his lip out and pouted like a child.

Mike excused himself to go to the bathroom. As soon as he was out of ear shot Lindsey shot a look at Kevin. "Could you at least try to get along? You didn't have to come if you didn't want to," she said.

"I am trying," Kevin defended.

"You are not. You're trying hard not to get along," Lindsey accused.

"What is that? How do you try not to get along?"

"By sitting there sulking and making yourself miserable. Why did you even come if you're so miserable?"

"Who said anything about being miserable? I'm not miserable. I'm having a great time. You're the one jumping to conclusions. I was minding my own business when you started your little hissy fit. Leave me alone, and I'll be fine," Kevin replied.

"Oh, don't hand me that bull. No one has to tell me you're miserable when you've been sitting there sulking all night. What are you sulking about?" Lindsey asked.

"I wasn't sulking. I am now because I'm getting my head chewed off for something I didn't do," Kevin answered.

Mike walked back up. "Do I need to give you a minute?" he asked.

"No. Everything's fine, Mike. I'm sorry. Please, sit down," Lindsey said politely.

Mike sat down and looked around uncomfortably for a minute. Kevin was glaring right at him. Lindsey kicked Kevin underneath the table, but it did not stop him from glaring at Mike.

"So, Lindsey, are you going to sing?" Mike asked.

"Me? Oh, no. Not a chance," Lindsey responded.

"I thought Rodney said you liked karaoke."

"Oh, I do. I love it, but I don't sing in public," Lindsey replied.

"Oh."

There was a minute of uncomfortable silence. Kevin was still glaring.

"Kevin, you don't like me very much, do you?" Mike came out and asked.

"If that's what you want to think, Mike, you go right ahead," Kevin said.

"Kevin!" Lindsey shrieked.

"What? It's a free country. Let him think what he wants," Kevin said.

"What is wrong with you? I'm sorry, Mike. I don't know what's gotten into him," Lindsey said.

"Don't apologize for me. If I were sorry, I'd say it, and nothing has gotten into me," Kevin shot off.

"Kevin!"

"No, Lindsey, it's ok. I'm an unfamiliar face in his territory. That can be intimidating. I'd do the same thing in his place," Mike said.

"Hold up. Let's get one thing straight right now. I am not intimidated by you or anyone else in this room. Don't compare me to you. You don't know what is bothering me. I would appreciate it if you quit pretending you do," Kevin snapped.

"Kevin, stop it!" Lindsey pleaded.

"You stop," Kevin responded.

"You're being childish. Just take me home," Lindsey ordered.

"Fine by me," Kevin said. He stood up and pushed his chair hard underneath the table.

They rode in complete silence until Kevin dropped Mike off at the hotel. "Lindsey," Kevin said.

"Shut up, Kevin," Lindsey shot back.

"If you'll just let me explain."

"There is no excuse. You acted like a spoilt two year old," Lindsey told him.

"Can't we talk about it?"

"No. I don't want to hear it," Lindsey insisted.

Kevin mumbled under his breath, "I was only jealous, because I love you," but Lindsey did not hear him.

Elizabeth Lee Sorrell

Chapter FOURTEEN

The next morning Lindsey got up early to go to the hotel and apologize to Mike. She did not know what room Mike was in, so she decided to wait in the lobby until he came down. She waited almost two hours. She was about to give up when she saw Mike. "Lindsey, what in the world are you doing here?" he asked.

"I wanted to apologize for last night. Mike, I'm so sorry. Kevin had no right acting the way he did. I don't know what his problem was. He's really not a bad guy. He's just been acting strange lately. I'm sorry you got put in the middle of that," Lindsey said.

"Don't worry about it. There was no harm done. Have you had breakfast yet?" Mike asked.

"Yeah, I ate before I left the apartment," Lindsey answered.

"That's too bad. I'll see you at the game though. Right? Maybe we can do something after the game," Mike said.

"That sounds great as long as Kevin doesn't come," Lindsey laughed.

Kevin moped around the field all afternoon. He never smiled. He hardly talked. He warmed up and did his own thing. Lindsey did not fool with him too much. She was still upset and embarrassed about the way he acted last night, and now he was pouting because he did not get his way. Lindsey was not about to cater to that.

Several people asked about Kevin's mood. Lindsey shrugged her shoulders and said, "I have no idea what's bothering him." It was the truth to an extent at least.

Lindsey met Mike back at the hotel after the game. "So, what did you have in mind?" Lindsey asked.

"Something within walking distance. I was beat this morning," Mike answered.

Mike and Lindsey started walking not sure where they were headed. They talked about this and that. They ended up not doing anything at all. They turned back towards the hotel still talking. When they got back to the hotel they stood outside still talking. Time flew by as they talked.

Lindsey glanced down at her watch. "Oh my goodness. It's nearly three. I better get out of here, so that you can get some rest," she said.

Mike leaned in and started to kiss her but pulled back. "I'm sorry. I shouldn't have..." he said trailing off.

Lindsey pushed up on her tiptoes and kissed him.

"Can I see you tomorrow... before the game?" he asked.

"I'd like that," Lindsey answered.

"Meet me for breakfast? Here, seven o'clock?"

Lindsey nodded.

Mike kissed her briskly. "Good night," he said.

"Good night."

When Lindsey got to the hotel that morning, Mike was waiting for her in the lobby. He smiled when he saw her walk in. He kissed her. "Tired?" he asked.

"Very," Lindsey responded.

"Sorry we had to meet so early. Get away day is kind of hectic. Well, you know," Mike said.

Lindsey nodded. Lindsey did know how hectic get away day could be, especially if you were out till three the night before. The Braves had one more series at home, and the Phillies had two more on the road. After breakfast, Lindsey went up to help Mike pack since he did not have time last night.

Everything was neatly in its place. The room looked picture perfect. Lindsey was not used to that. By get away day her hotel room looked frightful. Things would be strewn everywhere. She would come in after the games and throw her stuff wherever she could find a place. "You really are a neat freak. Aren't you?" Lindsey commented.

"I warned you," Mike reminded her.

"I have never seen a hotel room this clean, at least not when it's occupied. You could just about give this room the white glove test," Lindsey said.

"I don't know about a white glove, but I can't stand a mess," Mike admitted.

Because everything was so organized, it did not take long to get Mike packed up. "I think that's about it," Mike said.

"Yeah, that didn't take long at all. Maybe there's something to be said for neat freaks. You double check out here, and I'll double check the bathroom," Lindsey said.

She went and looked around the bathroom. She did not see anything they missed. "All clear," she called.

As she turned around to walk out, she ran right into Mike who was standing in the bathroom doorway. He had his arms stretched across the door frame.

"Oh," Lindsey said surprised. Mike leaned down and kissed her. He wrapped his arms around her waist and stopped to look at her.

"Are you going to tell Kevin?" he asked.

"Ugh. Do I have to?"

"If he doesn't hear it from you, he'll hear it somewhere else," Mike told her.

"I know, and I'm going to tell him. I am. I'm just dreading it," Lindsey sighed.

Mike kissed her. "I need to get to the ball park and see if I can get going before the game. Are you going to come to the airport and see me off?" he asked.

"Umm-hmm," Lindsey hummed and she kissed him.

Lindsey looked for Kevin everywhere when she got to the ball park. She finally spotted him across the field. He was off to himself. He had his bat and was taking practice swings. He looked mad already. Lindsey knew his mood would not get better anytime soon. "It's now or never," she whispered to herself and started across the field.

Kevin did not see her. He was in his own little world. Lindsey walked up beside him. "Kevin, I need to talk to you," she said.

"Oh, well," Kevin said and walked off.

Lindsey chased after him. "Kevin, wait. It's important," she called.

"That's too bad," Kevin replied and changed his direction.

"Kevin, please, would you just listen to me?" Lindsey called.

Kevin threw his bat down and turned around to face Lindsey. "I did listen to you. I actually listened. I even started to believe you. I kept thinking about what you said the other night about the way I acted. I started to feel bad. I went to the hotel this morning to apologize in person, but when I got there it looked like you had already done that for me. Imagine my surprise when I see the two of you standing in the lobby kissing. When did you plan to tell me, Lindsey? You could have said something instead of letting me find out like that," Kevin accused.

"That is what I'm trying to tell you right now," Lindsey defended.

"Well, it's a little late now," Kevin said, and he went to pick up his bat.

"Kevin, I'm sorry. I didn't mean for you to find out like that. It just sort of happened. I was going to tell you," Lindsey apologized.

"Save it, Lindsey. Things like that don't just happen. You've got to want it. You either let it happen or you don't," Kevin said and walked off.

Lindsey was still upset when she got to the airport. "Hey. What's wrong with you?" Mike asked.

"Kevin saw us this morning in the hotel lobby. He blew up when I tried to talk to him," Lindsey explained.

"This is hard for him. He'll calm down again. You'll see. Everything will be just fine. Just give him some time. He's not used to sharing you. Before I came along, he had all your time and attention. He's not used to sharing that. He'll come around," Mike assured her.

"I hope so. I hate seeing him like this. He's so grouchy," Lindsey replied.

"Hey, smile. Everything's going to turn out fine," Mike said. He kissed Lindsey. "I'll call you," he said, and he kissed her again.

Chapter Fifteen

Two weeks passed, but Kevin barely spoke to Lindsey. After another week, Kevin was speaking to her again, but he could not look her in the face. Lindsey had apologized a thousand times. She did not know what else to do.

They had one more series before the all-star break. They would play the Phillies in Philadelphia, then head to the all-star game. Kevin and Mike both made the all-star team. They would be expected to go to Pittsburgh and behave like teammates. Lindsey was not looking forward to the next week. She wanted more than anything to disappear.

Mike came to the airport to pick up Lindsey. Kevin was long gone as soon as he spotted Mike. After the first game of the series, Mike and Lindsey were going out with a few of Mike's teammates, but the first person Lindsey saw when they walked through the door was Kevin. He was sitting alone on the far wall with his back to the door. "Isn't there anywhere else we can go?" she asked Mike.

"Sure, how about somewhere quieter?" Mike replied.

"That would be perfect," Lindsey answered. Mike took Lindsey to a nice quiet restaurant that stayed open late where they ate outdoors underneath a full moon. It was very Lady and the Tramp like.

The next day Kevin avoided Lindsey and did a good job. Mike picked Lindsey up at the hotel that morning to take her to breakfast. They took their time eating and talking, and then headed to the field early. Lindsey knew Kevin was there somewhere, but she never once saw him until the start of the game. Afterwards Mike and Lindsey broke away from the group. They headed to a small all night café across town for drinks. They were hoping to avoid Kevin, but as soon as they pulled into the parking lot, there he sat. Lindsey could see him through the window. "Kevin's here," she told Mike.

"This is getting a little ridiculous, Lindsey," Mike commented.

"Can't we go back to your place?"

"Why not? What better place is there to hide?"

Lindsey hated making Mike feel that way, but she knew Kevin. She knew Kevin's temper, and she did not want to tempt fate.

There was nothing worth watching on TV. Mike pulled out an old movie and popped it in. Lindsey had no idea what he picked out. Not that it mattered, they were making out on the couch before the previews were over. Mike kept edging over. Before Lindsey knew what was going on, she was on her back with Mike on top of her.

Mike knew how she felt. He knew she was waiting until she got married to have sex, so she tried to ignore the overly sensual position. Things got pretty heated up. Lindsey felt Mike's hands wrap around her waist. That was ok. That felt good actually. As long as that was as far as he went everything was fine.

Mike and Lindsey kept going. Things continued to escalate. Mike started easing his hands inside Lindsey's shirt. "Mike... Mike stop... Mike," Lindsey called as she pushed him back. Mike sat up and jumped back to the other end of the couch.

"Lindsey, I'm sorry. I... Wow. I..." Mike responded.

"It's ok. You don't have to go way over there. I just want to slow down," Lindsey explained. Mike scooted over and started kissing her again. Then he sprung to his feet.

"Nope. Not going to work. I'd better take you back to the hotel," he said.

Mike met Lindsey at the hotel and they walked to breakfast the next morning. "How are you doing?" Lindsey asked.

"Oh, I made it though the night if that's what you mean. Let me tell you. Taking a cold shower, nothing but a myth," he teased. Lindsey laughed. They made it half way through breakfast when Kevin walked in.

"Mike," Lindsey whispered.

"No, Lindsey. No. We were here first. He did it to himself. Let him suffer," Mike argued.

Lindsey watched as Kevin was seated. He was alone. He sat down in perfect view of Mike and Lindsey's table. Mike's back was to Kevin, but Lindsey made clear eye contact with him. There was a look in Kevin's eyes that Lindsey had never seen before. It was a very serious almost threatening look.

"What is he doing?" Mike asked.

"Nothing. He's reading the menu," Lindsey answered. That was a lie. Kevin was looking dead at them, keeping constant eye contact with Lindsey.

"Why are you staring?" Mike asked.

"Am I?"

"Yes. You're staring. No wonder he's still so uncomfortable," Mike said. Since Mike was almost finished, Lindsey finished her breakfast as quickly as she could, and they left.

Mike and Lindsey went to Mike's house and got him packed for the all-star game. Then they went to the hotel and packed Lindsey, so they would be ready to go after the game.

Lindsey watched the two teams warming up. She noticed that Kevin kept looking over in Mike's direction. What was going through his head?

The Braves were ahead six to two in the top of the ninth. Kevin was up to bat when a wild pitch got away from the pitcher. It got him right in the knee. The ball hit going ninety-seven miles per hour. Lindsey leapt out of her seat as Kevin fell. He did not get up right away. It had to hurt. When Kevin was able to get up, he started walking it off and took his base, but he had a noticeable limp.

After the game Lindsey sent Mike on without her. "You go ahead. I want to check on Kevin. I'll meet you at the airport," she said. Then she kissed him and left.

Lindsey went straight to Kevin's room. She knocked on the door. "I'm packing. I'll be down in a minute," Kevin called.

"Kevin, it's me," Lindsey said. Kevin cracked the door.

"What's up?" he asked.

"I wanted to check on you. That was a nasty hit," Lindsey replied.

"I'm fine."

"You're lying," Lindsey accused.

"I'm not lying. I'm fine really."

"I know when you're lying. You're lying. What are you hiding? How bad is it? What's going on?" Lindsey asked in a near panic.

"Nothing, Lindsey. Why don't you come on in?" Kevin said as he opened the door. Lindsey walked in and he shut the door behind her.

There was a man sitting on the bed with a lap top. It was the same man Lindsey had met after Julio killed Aaron. Lindsey had heard Kevin refer to him as Ben several times. Ben was snickering from behind his lap top.

"Oh yeah, Kevin. You're still up for this case. You couldn't even lie to a reporter," he laughed. Then he looked up at Lindsey. "You did a good job, kid. Thank you," he said and winked.

Lindsey looked at Kevin. "What's he talking about?" she asked. Lindsey did not like the look on Kevin's face. He felt guilty about something, and she had an idea what. "Kevin, what have you done?" she cried.

"I'm sorry," he responded. Lindsey turned towards the door. She had to get to Mike. Kevin grabbed the tail of her shirt.

"Lindsey, wait," he said. Lindsey tugged out of his grip and ran out the door.

Lindsey looked down at her watch as she ran down the hallway. There was still two hours before they had to be at the airport, but she knew Mike would already be there waiting on her. She forgot all about her luggage and got to the airport as fast as she could. When she got there, she found Mike right away.

"Mike, Kevin's done something bad," she said running straight into his arms.

"He sure did, Lindsey," Mike responded. He grabbed Lindsey's arm and thrust a gun into her back. "My house is crawling with feds, Lindsey. Now how did that happen?" he asked. He snuck past an attendant before a security guard spotted them.

"Stop!" the guard yelled. Mike started to run dragging Lindsey along.

The guard drew his gun and started firing at them. Kevin ran into the terminal holding up his badge. "Hold your fire! This is a hostage situation. Hold your fire!" he screamed. Kevin took off, running after Mike and Lindsey.

Somehow Mike managed to scare enough people with his gun that he was able to get past all the securities put in place after nine-eleven. He pushed his way onto a plane ready to board still dragging Lindsey behind him. Kevin was still running after them, but Mike didn't seem to be paying him any attention.

Ben ran up to the first guard he saw. "Has that plane loaded yet?"

"No, sir," the guard answered.

"I need to know who's on that plane and how many."

"I don't know."

"You see that walkie talkie on your hip? You get on it and find me someone who does know," Ben said. "Now!" he shouted.

◆ ◆ ◆

Mike yanked Lindsey with him to the front of the plane. He walked into the cockpit and pointed the gun at the pilots. "Get this plane up in the air. Now! Move it. Let's go," Mike shouted. He yanked the radio down and waited until the plane was in the air. Then he went back and slung Lindsey into a seat. He sat down across from her as Kevin started sneaking up through the plane.

"So Kevin's a fed, huh?" Mike said. He shook his head. "Julio was involved with some bad men, Lindsey. Some real bad men who pay real well. I knew to check you out when you started asking all those nosey questions, but Kevin slipped right past me. I see it now. I don't know how I was so stupid. I was just beginning to care for you too. We really could have been great together. Tell me one thing, Lindsey. How did a sweet, innocent girl like you get mixed up in such a messy business?" Mike asked.

"I guess I just fall for all the wrong men," Lindsey answered nervously.

"I can see that being the case with you. I can. You do fall for the bad boys," Mike commented and kissed her forcefully. "Isn't it ironic? You keep falling for bad men like me when you've got a fed falling all over you. Oh, don't look so surprised, Lindsey. Kevin adores you.

Everyone but you knows just how much he loves you. Imagine it. A big, tough fed scared to tell you how he really feels. He'll never get the chance now. It's funny when you think about it. You loved him too. Didn't you? You'd be kidding yourself if you said no. I could see it in your eyes anytime he was around. You could never love me the way you loved him."

Another security guard walked up to Ben in the airport. "I'm Ross Stone, head of security," he said.

Ben held up his badge. "You're just the man I want to see, Stone. Tell me what I need to know," he said.

"There were two mechanics on board. The flight staff had been evacuated due to a gas leak. The mechanics were trying to locate the problem. Luckily for everyone those particular mechanics are highly skilled in flying that type plane. We lost transmission with the plane. We are currently trying to get a back up system up and running," Stone said.

"Show me, Stone. Show me. I have men on their way in the building to set up perimeter. I expect your men to stay out of the way. Your men have done enough damage missing that gun," Ben said.

Kevin was just behind Mike when he heard Ben say, "Hold all fire. There is a gas leak on the plane. I repeat hold all fire." Kevin looked down at the radio on his belt loop. Ben could be such an air head sometimes.

"Ah, Kevin, what an unexpected surprise. Come. Sit down. Join us," Mike said. Kevin walked around Mike slowly and carefully then sat down. "You're the fed, huh?" Mike asked.

"That's right. I'm the fed. I sent the men to your house. I pointed you out for the scum you are. Your beef is with me. Land the plane. Let the others go, and we'll settle this just you and me," Kevin negotiated.

"What others, Kevin? The pilots? They're good as dead. Lindsey? Why don't you let her decide? Maybe she doesn't want to go. Who's it going to be, Lindsey? Me or him?" Mike asked with the gun still pointed at Lindsey.

Lindsey sat there scared to answer. Her eyes darted in Kevin's direction for just a second.

"Unbelievable! There is a loaded gun pointed straight at you, and you're still going to choose him," Mike exclaimed.

"Mike, I'm only going to warn you once. I don't like it when people threaten her," Kevin said.

"Oh, I'm sure you don't," Mike replied.

"Mike, tell the pilots to land this plane."

"Or what, Kevin? You're going to kill me? Let me recap for you. I have a loaded gun. The plane has a gas leak, which makes my gun very explosive. One shot in any direction blows everyone sky high. That's not a chance you're willing to take with her life. Your own maybe, but not hers. I think this leaves me in control, so I call the shots, not you," Mike explained.

"Well, let's hear it. You're the captain where is this plane headed?" Kevin asked.

"Oh, I don't think so. You'd love me to tell you. Wouldn't you? Then you could get on your radio and have men waiting on me. Do I really look that stupid to you?" Mike asked.

"No. That's ok. Lindsey, where are we going?" Kevin asked.

Lindsey did not answer. She did not move. She did not make a sound.

"Lindsey, everything will be ok. No one is going to hurt you. Talk to me. Where are we going?" Kevin repeated.

"I... I don't know," Lindsey whimpered.

"Genius, Mike. You didn't tell the pilots where to go. Did you?" Kevin asked.

"I haven't decided yet," Mike replied.

"You better hurry up and decide. Ben didn't say what kind of leak. All he said was gas leak, kind of vague, don't you think? What if it's the fuel line? How far do you think we'll make it, Mike?"

Mike disappeared into the cockpit. Kevin put his hand on the back of Lindsey's head. "Are you ok?" he asked.

Lindsey nodded.

"Did he hurt you?"

Lindsey shook her head. "I'm scared," she whispered.

"It's ok to be scared, but I'm right here. Ok? I'm going to take care of you. Remember? I'm keeping a close eye on you. I'm not going to let anything happen to you. Hang in there a little while longer," Kevin told her.

"Well, it seems that we are going to crash now," Mike said. His clothes were covered in blood.

"What happened?" Kevin asked.

"The pilots decided that they would rather die than do what I told them. I thought that was a little rash, but they chose their own fate," Mike replied.

"Have you knocked out transmission with air control or am I safe in assuming that help is on the way?" Kevin asked.

"I'm not as stupid as you think, Kevin. I ripped the radio out before I ever left the cockpit. No one knows which way we're headed. You're on your own tough guy."

"Looks like I'm calling the shots again, Mike," Kevin said.

"How do you see that?"

"Unless you know how to fly this plane, you'll die in the crash too. You need help. We need someone to walk us though getting this plane back on the ground, and it sounds like my radio is the last working transmission with anyone down there," Kevin explained.

Mike started to pace. "That's one possibility. Or I could kill you, take your radio, and land this plane myself," Mike said.

"You could try."

"How's that knee, Kevin?" Mike asked.

"It's feeling pretty good, Mike. Do you want to see for yourself?" Kevin offered.

Mike eye balled a toolbox sitting in a seat. As he paced past the seat he reached in and grabbed a wrench.

"You know, Kevin, I think I do," Mike said. He turned around and came after Kevin with everything he had. The wrench slammed into Kevin's knee. Kevin screamed out in pain. He lunged after Mike but could not get any weight on his knee. Mike stepped back, and Kevin fell to the ground moaning. He grabbed at his knee.

Lindsey gasped still frozen in fear. She wanted to jump to her feet, run to Kevin's side, and check on him. She wanted to offer him comfort, but she couldn't make her frozen muscles to obey.

"Lindsey, get up and move to the back of the plane," Kevin instructed. He started pulling himself out of the floor. Kevin stood up on his right leg. Mike was several seats up watching Kevin struggle. Lindsey was caught right in the middle between Kevin and Mike. Lindsey was too scared to move. She did not know what Mike may do, and he was still so close to her.

"Lindsey, come on. Get out of here. Move it," Kevin ordered. Lindsey stood up using every bit of courage and will power she had in her.

"Sit down," Mike screamed.

"Lindsey, listen to me. Go," Kevin said. Lindsey stood frozen in fear.

"I don't think the two of you realize what's going on here. I have the upper hand. Kevin can't even stand up. Lindsey, think about it. Kevin can't help himself right now. He's not going to help you. He's not going to help anyone," Mike said.

"I've told you once," Kevin warned.

"Oh, that's right. You don't like it when people threaten Lindsey. Is this better? Lindsey, sit down or I'll use this wrench on you next," Mike threatened.

Kevin screamed as his left foot hit the ground. He yanked Lindsey into the isle and shoved her toward the back of the plane causing her to lose her footing and stumble to the floor. "Go," he growled. Then he tackled Mike. Lindsey scrambled to her feet. Mike and Kevin were rolling around fighting. Kevin's knee was getting slammed into the floor and the seats. Mike was right. Kevin could hardly stand. He needed help. Lindsey ran to the back of the plane. She started fumbling through things looking for anything she could use as a weapon.

Mike kicked Kevin's knee hard into one of the seats' hard metal legs. Kevin screamed out, and Mike shoved Kevin's head hard into the floor, knocking him unconscious. Blood started streaming from underneath Kevin's head. Mike jumped up and started searching for the wrench that Kevin had knocked loose. When Mike found the wrench, he busted Kevin's radio and headed for the back of the plane to find Lindsey.

Elizabeth Lee Sorrell

Chapter SIXTEEN

Ben heard static come in over the radio. He grabbed the radio. "Kevin?... Kevin, can you hear me?... Kevin!" he called. Ben turned to Ross Stone, the head of airport security. "Do we have contact with the plane yet?" he asked.

"No, sir," Stone answered.

"You better get contact now. This is no game. My brother is on that plane," Ben shouted. Then he turned to another FBI agent.

"Do we still have tracking on the girl?" he asked.

"Yes, sir," the agent answered.

"Thank heavens, the best decision Kevin ever made. Get a chopper, a plane, whatever it takes. Get Kevin off that plane. He's not going to die like that... NOW! Move it. Let's go get them down," Ben shouted.

◆◆◆

Lindsey found a gun, but she could not shoot it on the plane due to the gas leak. She grabbed the gun and kept looking. Lindsey found a first aid kit. She opened it hoping to find a pair of scissors or something she could use, but she did not have time. Mike walked in.

"Lindsey, what are you doing?" he asked.

Lindsey pointed the gun at Mike.

Mike laughed. "Do you even know what you're holding? That's a flare gun. Take a whiff, Lindsey. You can smell the gas fumes back here. Do you really think it would be wise to fire off a flare when you're surrounded by gas? Give me the gun, Lindsey," Mike said.

Lindsey did not move a muscle. She kept the gun pointed straight at Mike.

"Come on now, Lindsey. Don't do this. It doesn't have to be like this. I love you, Lindsey. Give me the gun," Mike urged.

"Where's Kevin?"

"Kevin's gone. It's just me and you now. We won't have to hide anymore. We can be together. Just give me the gun, Lindsey," Mike urged.

Kevin grabbed the back of his head. He was covered in blood. He got up and started limping quietly to the back of the plane.

◆◆◆

"What did you do to him?" Lindsey asked.

"Nothing, Lindsey, I swear. He did it to himself," Mike answered.

"Where is he?"

"Lindsey, it's too late for Kevin. It's just me and you now. I'm going to take care of you. We'll be happy together. Give me the gun," Mike pleaded.

Kevin eased behind Mike and pulled his gun. He hit Mike hard in the back of the head knocking him to the ground. Kevin pinned Mike down.

"I do not like people threatening her," Kevin said as he slammed Mike's head against the floor. "I do not like people busting my head," Kevin said and slammed Mike's head into the floor again. "And I do not like you, Mike," Kevin said.

He slammed Mike's head against the floor one last time. Then he drug Mike's body back to the seats, and he hand cuffed Mike's hands around one of the seats.

Kevin looked at Lindsey and shook his head. "A flare gun? Come on," he said. He grabbed his radio as he made his way to the cockpit.

"You're bleeding," Lindsey said.

Kevin ignored Lindsey and tried using the radio. It was soaked in blood and badly busted. "Ben... Ben, come in," Kevin called. There was no answer, and he threw the radio in frustration.

"Kevin?" Lindsey said.

"Not now, Lindsey. We've got to get this plane down," Kevin answered.

Lindsey screamed as they walked into the cockpit. One pilot was sitting in the seat slumped over the controls. Blood pooled across the plane's control panel. The other pilot lay in a corner. His body was beaten and mutilated. It looked like he had put up a fight before he died. He was swollen and bruised. Blood was all over the walls and the windshield. The whole scene was grotesque and frightening.

Kevin shoved the first pilot's lifeless body to the floor and sat down. "Oh," Lindsey moaned. "Can you fly this thing?"

"I don't know yet," Kevin replied.

"What do you mean you don't know yet? Have you ever flown a plane?" Lindsey asked.

"I've seen it done a million times," Kevin answered. He started fooling with knobs on the control panel and wiping blood away from gauges.

"Oh my goodness! What are you doing? What are you doing?" Lindsey asked in a very panicked voice.

"Lindsey, shut up. I'm trying to think. I've got to remember. I hate planes. They are nothing but trouble," Kevin complained.

"What are you talking about?" Lindsey asked still panicked.

"It's a long story with an ugly ending. Sit down and be quiet," Kevin responded. Lindsey did not sit down. The seat was soaked in blood. Everything was soaked in blood. The sight of the cabin and the two dead pilots made Lindsey sick to her stomach. She was scared. Her whole body shook with fear, and she started to cry.

"Kevin, what are you doing? What is that? What are you messing with?" she asked in a still more panicked voice than before. Her panic was rising with each passing second. "Oh my goodness. Oh my goodness. Oh my goodness. Oh my goodness," she chanted.

◆◆◆

This was hard for Kevin. He didn't know how to land a plane, and when it came down to it, he only had minimal knowledge of the workings of a plane. He needed to calm himself so that he could focus, yet he couldn't do that with Lindsey freaking out next to him. He had to distract her somehow.

"Lindsey, sit down and shut up!" Kevin shouted. Shocked Lindsey sat down. Kevin took a deep breath. "I'm sorry, but you've got to calm down. This is hard enough without you panicking. You need to focus on something else... I'm going to tell you a long story with an ugly ending. I need you to listen very carefully. Can you do that, Lindsey?" Kevin asked.

Lindsey nodded slowly with tears still streaming down her face.

Kevin needed Lindsey quiet long enough for him to concentrate. Digging up the past would not be easy, but Kevin hoped it would get Lindsey's attention.

"My dad was a pilot, and my mom was a flight attendant. Growing up my brother and I spent most of our lives on planes. I sat in the cockpit and watched my dad fly all the time. I don't think that was allowed, but no one ever told on us.

"Ben taught me to play baseball because my dad was always gone on another flight. He did not know all the in's and out's of the game, but he knew enough to get me started. As time passed, I got better, and I started showing Ben up on the baseball field. I didn't do it on purpose. Ben just didn't have the talent or love of the game that I did. Ben hated that I was better. He's got a problem with jealousy. I got the temper; he got the jealousy. There is almost ten years between me and Ben, but Ben's jealousy drove us further apart. We didn't always get along after that.

"I ended up going to college on a baseball scholarship. My major was still undecided my senior year. All I cared about was baseball. We went on to win the college championship that year. It all came down to the final game still evenly matched. My parents wouldn't have missed that game for the world. They traded flights so that they could be there for me. The flight they took crashed. It killed everyone aboard including both my parents.

"Ben immediately blamed me for their death. He said that if they hadn't traded flights to be at my game, they would still be alive today. Ben is older than me, and I've always looked up to him. So, when he said it was my fault, I believed him. I felt guilty after that. I felt worthless. I did not know what to do or where to go.

"Ben was the only family I knew. I followed him and did whatever he told me. He worked for the FBI, so I learned to. Ben taught me what I needed to know. I soaked it up fast. I got good at my job, and Ben's jealousy reared its ugly head. He kissed up and got a higher position. His position is not the right one for him, but he can say he's over me. That's all that matters, to believe he's better at something. He's better at a lot of things but not what he wants to be.

"It took me a long time to realize that what happened to my parents was not my fault, but I still to this day hate planes. Ben developed a phobia of planes. He will not ride in one. He will not set foot on one. He will not have anything to do with planes. They scare him to death. If you ask Ben today, he finally admits that it wasn't my fault. He said that he was grief stricken when he said that. He didn't mean any of it. He says that, but I don't believe it. When we were growing up, Ben and I were close. We were more than brothers. We were best friends. I wanted to be just like him. After my parent's death we were never close again. For Ben, I'm a burden. For me, Ben is my last hope at family. He loves me, and that's all I have left to hold on to.

"I will be out of his way soon. This was my last assignment. I should have lost my job a long time ago. I let my temper get the best of me too much. Ben has pulled strings every time my temper got me into trouble. Being spokesman for Forest Hills was the last string he had to pull. When this case came up, they needed someone who could pass for a major leaguer. I made a reputation in college for the way I played ball. A lot of scouts threw my name around. Ben used that to get me in. Once you've used your real name and been in the public's eye like I have, you're pretty much finished in the FBI unless you plan to take on a more public desk job. That isn't for me; I've never been one to stay put for long, too much energy, I guess. After this is all over, I'll have to learn to make it on my own without Ben," Kevin explained.

It worked. Lindsey was calm and quiet. Kevin was flying the plane. Unbelievable! Kevin was actually flying the plane.

◆ ◆ ◆

"I think I've got it," a man screamed from behind a computer. "Testing one, two. This is ground control. Do you copy?"

Ben rushed over. "How does it work?"

"Press and hold this. Then just talk," the man answered. It was like any other basic walkie talkie, child's play.

Ben pressed the button. "Kevin, can you hear me? Come back."

"Lindsey, did you hear that?" Kevin asked.

"Kevin, can you hear me? Come back."

"That's Ben! Lindsey, find where that's coming from," Kevin instructed. Lindsey started searching.

"Kevin, come back!" Ben said. Kevin looked around.

"Lindsey, push that. Push that red button there and hold it," he said. Lindsey pushed the red button and held it. "Ben," Kevin shouted. Lindsey released the button.

"Kevin! Thank heavens! What is going on up there?" Ben asked.

"I've got two dead mechanics. Mike is handcuffed to a seat, and I'm flying. Ben, I'm flying the plane just like Dad did, but I can't remember how to land. I always slept through the landing," Kevin admitted.

"Ok. Hang in there, Kevin. You're doing great. I'm going to find someone to talk you down," Ben said.

"Ok," came another voice. "You are right over a small airport. You should see the lights."

"I see them," Kevin answered.

"Great, the first thing you need to do is check the wind speed. It will be indicated in white."

"I see it."

"You need to keep your speed relatively in the middle of that speed. When you look out the windshield, so you see more land or more sky?"

"More land."

"Pull back on the stick until you see more sky. You're in a dive and need to level it up. I'm initiating auto pilot from here. It will bring you in until about one hundred feet from the ground. Hold on, and be ready to follow my instructions."

Kevin sat back and took a deep breath. There was sweat rolling down the sides of his face. He did not feel necessarily hot or cold, but there were chill bumps all along his arms. The hairs on his arms stood straight up on end. He watched straight out the windshield. He did not know what he was watching for, but he watched anyway.

Soon the runway was in full view and getting closer until it almost disappeared beneath the plane.

"Alright pull slightly up on the stick. Now push the stick forward until the front touches down. Then pull the throttles all the way back and step on the break."

Kevin continued to breathe evenly and followed directions like he was an old pro at flying planes. They landed safely. Mike was taken away by the FBI, and Kevin was rushed to the hospital. He had lost a lot of blood already. His knee was badly bruised, but luckily not broken. He also had to have eight stitches in the back of his head.

Chapter Seventeen

The doctors would not let Lindsey back to see Kevin that day. Ben was only allowed back for a brief few minutes.

"He's going to be just fine. I don't know why they won't let us back there. It's just a few stitches. It's not the first time that boy's had stitches, and I don't imagine that it will be the last. I guess they want to be sure... I was scared there for a while... I don't know if Kevin ever told you, but we lost our parents in a plane crash. I can't stand planes. I don't think I could stand to lose Kevin too, especially in a plane crash. Do you have any siblings?" Ben asked.

"No," Lindsey answered.

"Oh, it's wonderful, but what a responsibility when you're the oldest. I love that boy more than life itself. I couldn't forgive myself if I let something happen to him," Ben said.

The doctors told Lindsey that she could come back tomorrow. They would let visitors back to see Kevin first thing in the morning. Lindsey did come back. The doctors had let Ben back sometime during the night. It was late afternoon before Lindsey was allowed back.

"Can I come in?" Lindsey asked from the doorway. Kevin was laying in bed watching the all-star game on TV.

"Yeah, come on in. The national league is ahead. Pull you up a chair. You just missed Ben. He has a meeting with one of his superiors about a position better suited to his personality. It's actually a step up from where he is now. The most amazing thing happened. It's like every wall between me and Ben has been knocked down," Kevin said.

"That's wonderful. How are you feeling?" Lindsey asked.

"Oh, I feel fine. My knee is a little sore, but I should be getting out of here soon," Kevin replied.

It was hard seeing Kevin in a hospital bed. He had always been this pillar of strength before. Lindsey could see now that she had actually thought of him as impenetrable. In her mind he had, in some ways, become a super hero. It went against the grain to think of him as hurt and helpless. It was scary and painful to think of him that way.

"What are you going to do when you get out?" Lindsey asked.

"Now that I'm out of the FBI? I don't know yet," Kevin answered.

"Have you ever thought about making baseball your career?"

"Lindsey, come on. We both know the FBI got me that position."

"They may have got you the job, but you earned your position," Lindsey replied. He was crazy if he thought otherwise, and the

Braves would be crazy to give him up. He was an asset to the team and to the community.

Kevin blew the idea off as impossible.

Lindsey stayed and watched the game with Kevin. The national league fell behind and lost, which meant that the American League would have home field advantage at the World Series.

"I've got to get back to Atlanta. Take care of yourself," Lindsey said. The last thing she wanted to do was to leave Kevin there. It almost felt like she was abandoning him, but that was ridiculous. His brother would be there for him, and he needed time to heal. Besides, Dan would love any excuse to fire Lindsey as the Braves liaison.

Still, leaving Kevin lying in a hospital bed was the hardest thing she had ever done. As she walked out, Ben walked in. He turned and watched her walk out of sight. Then he walked over to Kevin's bed.

"Did you tell her?"

"Tell her what?" Kevin replied.

"That you love her."

Kevin shook his head. She'd had such bad luck with men. He couldn't blame her if she decided to write men off after what happened with Mike. If Kevin told her how he really felt only to be rejected... No, it was better this way. Not knowing was easier.

"You may have got all the talent, but I got all the brains in this family. What's stopping you?"

"I've never felt this way about anyone before. What if she doesn't feel the same?"

"Kevin Baxter, are you telling me that you are scared of a little ol' girl?" Ben teased.

"No. I'm telling you that I'm petrified of a little ol' girl," Kevin laughed.

Chapter Eighteen

The Braves started back with two series at home. Nothing was the same without Kevin there. Lindsey missed him terribly. Everyone wanted to know about what happened. Ben had briefed Lindsey at the hospital on what to say. He told her what answers to give and what answers to withhold. Lindsey stuck strictly to the script she had been given. She had very little time for interviews in between everyone questioning her.

One thing Lindsey wanted to know, who was planned to replace Kevin on a more permanent placement. For now, utility players were filling in the gaps and doing a good job. They were no Kevin, of course, but they were getting the job done. Still, Lindsey was curious and continued to ask around. Everyone said the same exact thing. Their response was better rehearsed than Lindsey's. "Don't know. Whoever it is, they'll be here when we get back from the road trip."

The Braves had a three stop road trip following the two series at home. That would be almost two and a half weeks down the road. That was a horribly long time to wait for a replacement. There was someone up from the minors to fill in temporarily, but no one had been announced as a permanent replacement. It was good to get a little experience in the show, but Lindsey was anxious to move on to the next step. She knew it was a given that Kevin wasn't coming back; there would have to be a permanent replacement. It was strange that the Braves were waiting so long to make a decision on the next move. Something was out of place.

Finally, rumors started floating around that a replacement would meet them in Atlanta for the next home series. Lindsey was overly anxious to get back home after the road trip. She could hardly wait to find out who was going to try filling Kevin's shoes.

It didn't matter anyway. They would have large shoes to fill, and as far as Lindsey was concerned, it couldn't be done. Kevin was an outstanding player and an outstanding friend. She was going to miss him, terribly.

The first game back in Atlanta, Lindsey got to the ball park bright and early. She was nearly one of the first ones there. The players started trickling in. Lindsey interviewed one after another, but no one would talk about Kevin's replacement. Lindsey was interviewing the catcher and getting nowhere.

"Be honest with me. You do know who's going to be playing right field on a more permanent basis. Don't you?" she urged.

"Maybe," the catcher answered.

"Can't you give me at least a hint?" Lindsey nudged.

"He's right over there. Why don't you go interview him?" the catcher replied.

Lindsey looked across the field in the direction the catcher was pointing, and saw Kevin standing there. Lindsey took off running across the field. She leapt into Kevin's arms and wrapped her arms around him. "Kevin! What are you doing here?" she exclaimed.

"You're looking at the Braves new right fielder. I got the job all on my own," Kevin replied.

Kevin and Lindsey became inseparable the second half of the season. Although nothing was official, it was an understood thing around the ball club that Lindsey was off limits.

Late one night, Kevin and Lindsey were watching a movie at his house. They were sitting on the couch. Lindsey was curled up in Kevin's arms, and she looked asleep. Kevin kissed the top of her head, careful not to wake her. "I love you," he whispered quietly.

"I love you, too," she replied. From that moment on there was no doubt in anyone's mind that Kevin and Lindsey were dating and were very serious.

The Braves made it to play in the World Series against the Yankees in New York. They went to game seven tied up.

Two of the game's toughest pitchers went head to head. In the bottom of the ninth there was still no score. The pitchers had pitched their hearts out and had nothing left. The bullpen came in for both teams and pitched another flawless inning.

The game went on to the eleventh. A base hit followed by a double drove in Atlanta's first run, but in the bottom of the eleventh, the Yankees matched Atlanta's run with a solo home run. The game drug on through the twelfth, thirteenth, and fourteenth innings still tied one, one. In the fifteenth Atlanta's lead off man got on with a single. The second batter followed with a double. The Yankees issued the first walk of the game to the Braves' catcher bringing Kevin to the plate with the bases loaded. Kevin watched three balls go past. Then on the fourth pitch Kevin hit a grad slam giving Atlanta the lead five to one.

Atlanta's outstanding defense held the Yankees in the bottom, and the Braves won the World Series after fifteen innings, five to one.

Kevin's grand slam drove in the winning runs for the World Series. Of course, afterwards everyone went to celebrate. It was very loud with all the cheering and hollering. You could not hear one another at all. Kevin leaned in and said something into Lindsey's ear. She could not hear him, but she knew exactly what he had said when he showed her an engagement ring. Lindsey kissed him, and Kevin slipped the ring on her finger.

About THE Author

Elizabeth Lee Sorrell is an Alabama native. A gifted teacher, she has worked with babies and preschoolers, from her teens all the way to today. She is a teacher in the Federal Head Start program. She has her Associate's Degree in Early Childhood Development, her Bachelor's in Early Childhood Education and Elementary Education, and her Master's in Early Childhood Education.

When not teaching, or leading as the Nursery Coordinator of her church, she is with her family and dear friends, probably reading or writing a book. She loves to spend time with her nieces. Elizabeth is a Christian. She cheers for the Auburn Tigers, and the Atlanta Braves. As a big baseball fan, she has, more than once, written stories in the world of MLB, and watches as many games as she is able.

She enjoys pairing up with Sandra JS Coleman for her covers and illustrations. Sandra, Elizabeth's sister, is a graphic designer and an illustrator.

Learn more at www.ElizabethLeeSorrell.com

Colophon

Cover Design, Cover Photography, and interior
layout designed by Sandra JS Coleman using
Adobe CC software. She is the graphic designer and
illustrator for Yarbrough House Publishing Inc. Sandra lives in
North Alabama with her husband and daughter.

The typefaces used on the cover and interior are
Alamq, Garamond Premier Pro, and Chantel.

The book was printed in the United States of America, on 50lb white
paper, perfect bound, with a gloss color cover.

www.ingramcontent.com/pod-product-compliance
Lightning Source LLC
Chambersburg PA
CBHW071412100726
47908CB00004B/1150